Akiko

in the Castle of Alia Rellapor

Poog

Gax

Akiko

Mr. Beeba

Spuckler

in the Castle of Alia Rellapor

Written and illustrated by
MARK CRILLEY

A DELL YEARLING BOOK

35 Years of Exceptional Reading

Dell Yearling Books
Established 1966

Published by
Dell Yearling
an imprint of
Random House Children's Books
a division of Random House, Inc.
1540 Broadway
New York, New York 10036

Visit us on the Web! www.randomhouse.com/kids

Educators and librarians, for a variety of teaching tools, visit us at
www.randomhouse.com/teachers

ISBN: 0-440-41657-4

Reprinted by arrangement with Delacorte Press

Printed in the United States of America

November 2002

10 9 8 7 6 5 4 3 2 1

OPM

For my parents-in-law,
Kouji and Minae Hirabayashi

ACKNOWLEDGMENTS

I'd like to belatedly acknowledge the ongoing influence of David Small, not just upon this book, but upon all my endeavors as a writer and illustrator. I'd also like to express deep gratitude to my editor Fiona Simpson, who shepherded this book through from beginning to end, as well as Jennifer Wingertzahn, who has kindly volunteered to pick up where Fiona left off. Thanks as always to Robb Horan, Larry Salamone, and Mark Bellis of Sirius Entertainment, and to Melissa Knight, Alison Kelly, and everyone else at Random House who helps me with my work. And, finally, big hugs and kisses to Miki and Matthew, who graciously put up with me spending far too many hours hidden away in the basement working on this book.

chapter 1

The snow crunched loudly beneath our feet. Spuckler Boach was out in front, whistling a cheerful little tune, while Mr. Beeba huffed and puffed along, great clouds of breath trailing behind his bright yellow tufts of hair. Poog, his custom-made coat snugly concealing most of his round little body, floated steadily by my shoulder like some kind of alien bodyguard. And just behind me, rolling and squeaking over the surface of the snow on his four rusty wheels, was Spuckler's robot, Gax. We must have made a pretty funny-looking group.

The morning sky was a bright, cloudless blue. It

stretched from snow-covered hills on one side of us to jagged purple peaks on the other. Judging by the steep incline of the road, we were heading into the mountains. A bracing cold breeze blew directly into our faces, making me wish we could head in the opposite direction and somehow still get where we wanted to go.

"There ain't nothin' like fresh mountain air," Spuckler said. "Really gets the blood curdling!"

"Curdling?" Mr. Beeba wheezed. "I don't know *what* word you're searching for, Spuckler," he added, gasping for breath, "but it's surely not *curdling.*"

"Yeah, whatever," Spuckler replied.

Lacking the energy to join in the argument, I stayed quiet and just let my thoughts roll around in my head. I couldn't think of anything else to do, so I decided I'd try to figure out how many days I'd been here on the planet Smoo.

Let's see, now . . .

Bip and Bop came to get me at my bedroom at eight P.M., and I arrived at King Froptoppit's palace in the middle of the night, so I figured that didn't count as a real day. Maybe a quarter of a day?

Skip it.

The first *real* day was when the journey began. That was when the King introduced me to Mr. Beeba and Poog, and we picked up Spuckler and Gax, and then we flew off in the ship and got into all that trouble with the Sky Pirates. Man, what a crazy way to get started. Me, Akiko, face to face with a fire-breathing lizard! The kids in my fourth-grade class back on Earth would never believe it in a million years.

Okay, so that was one day.

The next day, hmmm . . .

. . . Oh yeah, we got swallowed up by the giant water snake on our way to the Sprubly Islands. That was the same day Mr. Beeba and Spuckler went off into the forest and left me all alone with Poog and Gax. Wow, that already seemed like *ages* ago.

That made two days.

Okay, so the next day we went to the palace of Queen Pwip in the morning and then climbed the Great Wall of Trudd in the afternoon. That made three. And yesterday we crossed over that superlong bridge, ran right smack dab into Throck, and wound up sleeping around a campfire.

That was four days all together. That meant today was the fifth day.

Five days? Was that all? I don't know, it didn't even seem *possible* that we could have done so much in just five short days.

"We're comin' up to some kind of a ridge here," Spuckler said.

My mind snapped back to attention. Spuckler was ten or fifteen feet ahead of me, quickly marching to a point where the white road met the bright blue sky. I moved my legs as fast as I could to keep up with him.

"This might be it."

It? Alia Rellapor's castle?

A shiver ran through me. Part of me wanted to turn around and run back downhill as fast as I could, but I forced myself to keep moving forward.

Calm down, I told myself. This is no time to panic.

My mind was spinning with questions. Would we be able to rescue Prince Froptoppit? Would we even be able to *find* Prince Froptoppit? Would we run into that creep Throck again? And then there was Alia Rellapor. Would we finally confront her in person?

"Yeah, guys," said Spuckler. "I'm almost *sure* this is it."

"Don't get our hopes up, Spuckler," Mr. Beeba gasped out between noisily drawn breaths. "You said the very same thing at the last ridge, and all we came to was several more miles of snow-encrusted road!"

"I'm tellin' ya, Beebs," Spuckler called back as he quickened his pace, "I got a feeling about this!"

"You and your feelings!" Mr. Beeba griped. "If we still had my *maps*, we'd have much more to go on than your feckless, fickle feelings!"

"VERY IMPRESSIVE ALLITERATION, SIR," Gax's tinny voice announced from the back of the group.

"Why, thank you, Gax," Mr. Beeba said with a grin, turning his head back to give Gax a wink. "I was rather pleased with it myself!"

I craned my neck, trying to get a peek at what lay beyond the ridge. All I could see was a range of mountains, purple and white in the distance. But as we plodded forward, I saw something tall and pointy, too perfect-looking to be a simple outcropping of stone.

"Spuckler," I called, pointing with an icy finger. "What *is* that?"

"I dunno, 'Kiko," he answered. "It's kinda funny-lookin', ain't it?"

We kept moving, gradually speeding up in our eagerness to figure out what we were seeing. As we made our way to the top of the ridge, the tall, pointy thing revealed itself to be a stone tower. It was covered with detailed carvings, like the surface of a Mayan temple. The closer we went, the more we could make out. Eventually we saw a second tower a little farther to the right. Then two more towers over on the left. Every step we took seemed to reveal the top of another tower, until finally it dawned on me: All the towers were part of a single building. *Alia Rellapor's castle!*

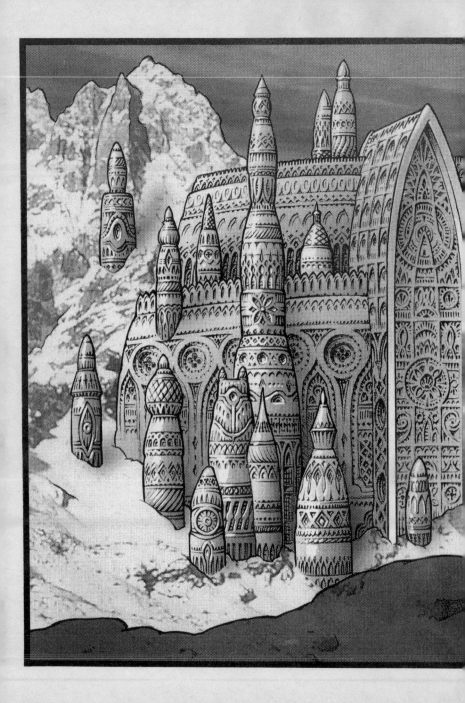

Chapter 2

Spuckler was the first to get to the top of the ridge. He rested his hands on his hips and shook his head slowly back and forth.

"Hot dang!" he cried, following it up with a pro-longed high-pitched whistle. "That is one heckuva *place* she's got there!"

I took the last few steps up to stand beside him and stood there gaping at the sight. Rising majestically from the side of an enormous snow-capped mountain, the castle was the size of an entire city. It was a mass of towers and walls, covered with alien decorations and ornate, soaring windows like the ones in a Gothic cathedral. It was scary and inviting and ugly and beautiful all at the same time. I'd never seen anything like it before, and I'm sure I never will again.

I glanced over at Poog, who was gazing at the castle with a strange, distant look in his eyes. It was almost as if he'd been there before and was familiar with every nook and cranny of the place. He wasn't smiling, but he wasn't exactly frowning, either. He was just really . . . I don't know, *serious*.

"Astonishing!" Mr. Beeba wheezed, bent over with his hands on his knees. "I don't believe I've *ever* seen such a hideous mishmash of architectural styles!"

"It's . . . ," I began, struggling to come up with a decent adjective. I gave up after a minute, sighed, then just said, ". . . amazing."

"All right, folks, we didn't come all this way just to enjoy the view," Spuckler said. "Let's march on down there and find a way inside."

"YOU MAKE IT SOUND SO EASY, SIR," Gax squeaked, rattling a bit in the frigid wind.

"Yes, Spuckler," Mr. Beeba agreed. "It won't be a simple matter of strolling up to the front door and ringing the bell. There's no telling what sort of sentinels Alia has dispatched to guard this fortress. We'll be putting our lives in peril merely attempting to go anywhere *near* the place."

"Yeah, well, we've managed to get *this* far," Spuckler retorted with a grin. "No sense gettin' cold feet now."

I swallowed hard and followed Spuckler as he strutted down the road leading to the castle. Mr. Beeba, Poog, and Gax joined us, looking no more eager to get inside that castle than I was.

The mountains with their snowy peaks rose menacingly all around us as we moved farther and farther down toward the castle. I stumbled once or twice on the stony path and found myself thinking of something my dad once told me about mountain climbing. He was born and raised in a small mountain village in Japan, and he always claims he had to climb a mountain every day just to get to school. I find that a little hard to believe (especially because my mom gives me a wink every time he says it), but he swears it's true. I don't know, maybe it was just a *small* mountain.

Anyway, he told me that climbing *down* a mountain is

just as hard as climbing *up* one, and that sometimes it can be even more dangerous. People going down a mountain can start to move too fast if they're not careful. Then if they take just one bad step—

"Spuckler!" Mr. Beeba called out, interrupting my thoughts. "Look down there to the right. Those are Torg patrols, aren't they?"

"Good eyes, Beebs," Spuckler answered, stopping in his tracks.

I tried to get a look at what Mr. Beeba was talking about, but all I could see were these little gray dots in the distance.

"Torg patrols?" I asked.

"The word *Torg* is an acronym, Akiko," Mr. Beeba explained. "It stands for *Turbo Obtuvian Retramodular Gigatron.*"

There was a very long pause.

"Torg patrols?" I asked again.

"They're general-use robots," Spuckler said, as if he were translating for Mr. Beeba. "They can be programmed to do almost anything. Why, this whole castle was prob'ly *built* by Torgs."

GA-GUNCH! GA-GUNCH!

Suddenly we heard a loud mechanical sound coming from somewhere below us, the sound of a gigantic piece of machinery. From behind a large boulder to our left, an enormous gray robot lurched out into the middle of the road only fifty or sixty feet ahead of us.

GA-GUNCH! GA-GUNCH!

"Heavens!" Mr. Beeba squealed. *"A T-t-torg!"*

chapter 3

Spuckler hurried us all off the road to a spot behind an enormous slab of stone. We crouched down and huddled together, hoping we weren't visible from the road. The noise kept getting louder.

GA-GUNCH! GA-GUNCH!

Spuckler had his head poked out so he could keep an eye on the thing.

"It's gettin' closer," he whispered back to us.

"Get back here and keep quiet!" Mr. Beeba whispered. "Maybe it didn't see us."

"I never been much for hidin'," Spuckler whispered back through gritted teeth. "Makes me feel like a sissy."

"Come on, Spuckler," I said, reaching out to grab him by the arm. "Stay here and hide with us, just this once."

GA-GUNCH! GA-GUNCH!

"Sorry, 'Kiko," Spuckler said as he pulled himself free. "Gotta take her on face t' face. It's the only way I know."

Mr. Beeba groaned as we watched Spuckler swagger out into the middle of the road. I couldn't see the robot yet, but I could tell it was pretty close. Spuckler folded his arms and stood in the middle of the path like a statue. Gax shuddered and wheezed a little. I wondered if he'd ever had to deal with a Torg before.

FZAMM!

Just then a bolt of yellow light shot past Spuckler and struck a boulder a few feet behind him. My jaw dropped as I stared at the enormous hole it left in the rock. Spuckler wasn't fazed a bit.

By now the Torg had come into full view. It was about thirty feet tall, with two enormous legs and six spindly mechanical arms hanging off its body. The entire surface of the robot was pale gray, with spots of white frost. It leaned forward and raised an arm, a double-jointed one with a smoking laser gun at the end. There was a rapid clicking sound as it prepared to shoot again.

Spuckler leaned over and picked up a small stone. He snapped his hand back and chucked the stone up at the robot's body.

TWING!

There was a tinny whistling sound like a ricocheting bullet in a Western movie. Spuckler grimaced and leaped to one side as a second bolt of yellow light shot past him, this time missing by just a few inches.

"Heavens," Mr. Beeba whispered to me. "One more shot and he'll be vaporized for sure!"

"*V-vaporized?*" I gasped.

"It's actually not such a bad way to go, Akiko," he whispered. "Virtually painless, in theory . . ."

FLAM!

Spuckler flipped backward, just barely dodging a third laser bolt. He reached down and picked up another rock. This time he paused, like a pitcher trying to throw his best fastball. He let the rock fly.

TWACK!

Suddenly there was a horrible groaning sound, followed by a series of loud pops. Little orange sparks shot out from the spot where the stone had hit, dropping to the snow like brightly colored confetti. The giant robot heaved and shuddered, rocking violently from side to side. Then, all at once, it simply screeched to a halt. A second or two later its six arms twitched briefly, then just hung there, squeaking quietly in the chilly breeze.

"Nice *shot*, Spuckler!" Mr. Beeba said, rising to his feet.

"You did it!" I cried, running out to give Spuckler a big hug. Poog smiled, and Gax buzzed happily. He seemed very proud of his master.

"Tell me, Spuckler," Mr. Beeba continued. "How did you know where his weak spot was?"

"Well, I used to work in a Torg repair shop when I was younger," Spuckler answered, brushing snow off his arms and legs. "They ain't nearly so scary when ya know how lousy the engineerin' is."

We all stepped out into the middle of the path to get a better look at the giant, motionless Torg.

"Hang on now, everybody," Spuckler said as he fumbled around in Gax's little junk container. "I gotta make sure he's permanently deactivated before we move on. Don't want him springin' back to life later on an' alertin' the other Torgs . . ."

He pulled out a pair of wire cutters and squeezed the handles. They made a rusty scraping sound.

"Yeah, these'll do the trick," Spuckler said. He tucked them behind his belt and began shinnying up one of the Torg's legs.

"SIR, IF I MIGHT MAKE A SUGGESTION," Gax said as politely as he could.

"Gax, I know it ain't easy to see a fellow machine bite the dust like this," Spuckler said as he hoisted himself on top of the robot's body, "but I gotta do what I gotta do."

"BUT SIR, IT SEEMS TO ME THAT—" Gax began in a slightly louder voice.

"It'll all be over in a second, Gax," Spuckler interrupted as he pulled a bunch of wires out of the base of the robot's head and prepared to sever them all with a single snip.

"WILL YOU JUST *LISTEN* TO ME FOR ONCE IN YOUR LIFE?" Gax screeched as loudly as his mechanical voice could manage (which was actually quite loudly).

Spuckler froze, an expression of shock and dismay on his face. Mr. Beeba and I exchanged astonished glances. None of us had ever heard Gax raise his voice to Spuckler before. Even Poog looked surprised.

The wind whistled past as we watched to see what would happen next. Spuckler's shock slowly gave way to an expression of barely contained fury.

"All right, Gax," he said between clenched teeth. "I'm listenin'."

Gax rattled and shuddered a bit. The wind died down. It became very, very quiet.

"I'm listenin' *real* good," Spuckler continued. "Now, supposin' you tell me what's goin' through that rusty little head of yours?"

Chapter 4

"WELL, SIR," **GAX** began, sounding much less sure of himself than he had only seconds before, "YOU MAY BE AWARE THAT I AM CONVERSANT IN THE TORG PRO- GRAMMING DIALECT. . . ."

"I am *now*," Spuckler growled.

"SO," Gax continued, cocking his head slightly to one side, "I BELIEVE THAT I COULD USE MY KNOWLEDGE OF THE TORG'S LANGUAGE TO REPROGRAM ITS NAVIGA- TIONAL CONSOLE, INSTRUCTING IT TO TAKE US INTO ALIA RELLAPOR'S CASTLE."

"Oh, that's a real humdinger of a plan, Gax," Spuck- ler sneered. "And what are we supposed to do? Walk behind it and wave to all the other robots we pass along the way?"

"NO, SIR," Gax answered, sounding slightly more confident. "WE'D ALL BE *INSIDE* THE TORG."

"Inside?" Spuckler asked, scratching his head.

"INSIDE THE STORAGE COMPARTMENT, SIR," Gax replied matter-of-factly. "BEHIND HIS HEAD. THERE SHOULD BE ENOUGH SPACE TO HOLD ALL OF US."

"But—" Spuckler began.

"That's a good idea, Gax," I interrupted, looking up to see that Poog was also smiling his approval.

"It's an *excellent* idea, Gax!" Mr. Beeba cried, clapping his big hands together. "It's an inspired strategic move of the highest order. Why, you should tell Spuckler to shut up more often, I say!"

Spuckler glared at Mr. Beeba, growling like an angry dog. He lowered the wire cutters, though, and turned to Gax with a humble expression on his face.

"All right, Gax. We'll give it a try."

Spuckler and Gax spent the next half hour or so reprogramming the Torg. The two of them mumbled about this circuit and that memory bank, occasionally

arguing but always sounding like old friends. I may have been imagining things, but I'd swear Spuckler sounded more respectful now when he spoke to Gax.

Mr. Beeba, Poog, and I kept a lookout from behind a boulder at the edge of the path. Luckily all the rest of the Torgs were down near the base of the castle, marching back and forth like little windup soldiers. I kept looking at Alia's castle with all its towers and turrets and Gothic arches. I wondered what it would be like to actually get inside that place. Where was Prince Froptoppit being held? I pictured him in a dark cell, with nothing but bread and water to eat all day.

"Don't worry, Prince Froptoppit," I said to myself. "We're almost there."

"All right, gang!" Spuckler called out from his perch on top of the Torg. "We're ready to roll!"

"This is going to be cool," I said as I climbed up one of the Torg's legs. "I've never been inside a robot before!"

"What's *happened* to you, Akiko?" Mr. Beeba asked disapprovingly. "You used to be such a *sensible* girl!"

Spuckler opened the large storage compartment on top of the Torg's body and we all climbed in. I immediately noticed a strong unpleasant smell, like burned rubber or diesel fuel. There were strange pieces of equipment crowded inside, but we managed to find enough space for all of us. Gax was near the front. Spuckler had connected a thick cable from Gax's body to the back of the Torg's head. I figured they'd rigged it so that Gax could program thoughts right into the

Torg's robotic brain. Mr. Beeba, Poog, and I huddled near the back of the compartment, sandwiched between two large metal crates. When we had gotten as comfortable as possible, Spuckler pulled the hatch down so that just a tiny sliver of light remained in the front.

"All right, Gax," Spuckler said. "Do your stuff!"

Gax clicked and whirred a bit and suddenly the Torg's engine roared to life. We heard a deep buzzing-humming noise, and the sound of gears turning just beyond the walls of our compartment.

GREEEEEEEEEE!

There was a high-pitched screech and the Torg lurched forward, then immediately came to an abrupt halt. We were all flung from the back of the compartment to the front, and I felt my face pressing into Spuckler's leathery coat.

"SORRY, EVERYONE," Gax squeaked. "MAKING THIS TORG WALK IS GOING TO REQUIRE A BIT OF PRACTICE."

"Take your time, Gax," I said, trying to sound as encouraging as I could. "I know you'll get the hang of it soon."

We all held our breath as Gax prepared to make the Torg move a second step.

GREEEEEEEEEE!

The Torg lurched forward again, this time taking three quick steps like a tiptoeing ballerina. We all bounced up and down, banging our heads on the underside of the hatch and bruising our bottoms on the cold metal floor.

"Come on, Gax," Spuckler said, moving his mouth right up next to Gax's head like a boxing coach in the ring. "Think *Torg*."

"I'M *TRYING*, SIR," Gax replied. "I'M JUST NOT USED TO THIS CONCEPT OF HAVING *LEGS*."

Chapter 5

After a few more false starts, Gax finally began to move the Torg forward step by step at a fairly steady pace. I imagine the giant robot must have looked like a one-year-old who'd just learned to walk. Thankfully I don't think any other robots saw us at this point. Ten or fifteen minutes later Gax had the Torg walking around like an old pro.

Gax instructed the Torg to walk down to the castle and find an entrance. I waited and watched as we caught glimpses of scenery through the nearly closed storage hatch. I'd see a sliver of the morning sky or a slice of the castle itself, growing ever larger as we approached it.

Eventually I saw other Torgs, stalking back and forth among the snow-covered boulders at the base of the castle. One of them crossed our path just a few feet in front of us, and we very nearly smashed right into it.

"SORRY ABOUT THAT," Gax said. "A RATHER CLOSE CALL, WASN'T IT?"

Mr. Beeba made a sound that was a cross between a sigh and a moan.

Finally we arrived at the front entrance of the castle. It was an enormous iron gate held in place by an ornate stone archway, with two flickering torches on either side. At the very top, in the exact center of the arch, a tiny robotic camera perched on the end of a short mechanical arm. It clicked and buzzed, apparently focusing intently on us.

"It's a surveillance robot," Spuckler explained. "It decides who gets to come in and who doesn't. With any luck the li'l feller's been programmed to 'open sesame' for any Torg that comes along."

With any luck. Well, it just wasn't our day.

GRICKLE-SPRICKLE-BOK-BOK!

The little camera vibrated, producing a series of

strange mechanical noises. It sounded like a hyperactive pinball machine.

MIRKLE-BIRKLE-CHEEK-CHEEK-CHEEK!

"What's going on?" I asked, leaning forward to get a better look.

"HE'S SCOLDING ME," Gax explained. "HE SAYS I WAS SUPPOSED TO BE BACK HERE HALF AN HOUR AGO."

"Quick!" Spuckler whispered. "Somebody come up with a good excuse!"

There was a short pause as we all struggled to think of something.

"I've got it!" Mr. Beeba said excitedly. "Tell him you were admiring the morning sunlight . . . as it cascaded upon the newly fallen snow . . . and you were so enchanted by it that you lost all track of time!"

"Robots are *machines*, you idiot!" Spuckler snapped. "They don't *do* stuff like that!"

"Er . . . enjoying the fresh mountain air, perhaps?"

Spuckler smacked Mr. Beeba soundly on the forehead, making a noise like a thumped pumpkin.

"I've got an idea," I said. "What if you say your navigation circuits blew out and you had trouble finding your way back to the castle?"

There was a moment of silence as Spuckler, Mr. Beeba, and Gax all turned to me with stunned expressions. Even Poog looked impressed, as if he hadn't expected this out of me.

"Now *that*," Spuckler said with an upraised finger, "is an *excuse*."

"Well done, Akiko," Mr. Beeba said, grinning enviously.

"Go on, Gax," Spuckler said. "Tell it to the robot, exactly like Akiko said."

Gax shivered a bit, and a moment later noises began to come out of the Torg's head.

NIRKLE-GIRKLE-DOK-DOK. DIRKLE-DIRKLE-GWEEEEK!

There was a long pause. The camera robot stayed motionless, its lens still pointed at us. It moved slowly back and forth, then made a brief mechanical noise.

KIRKLE-POTCH!

"Well?" Mr. Beeba asked.

"HE SAYS IT'S THE WORST EXCUSE HE'S EVER HEARD," Gax translated.

Nevertheless, there was a loud rumbling-groaning noise, followed by a piercing rusty screech, and the iron gate slowly began to rise. A moment later the passage-way was wide open, and Gax was able to make the Torg march inconspicuously into the castle.

Spuckler pushed the hatch open a bit farther so we could get a better look at our surroundings. We were in the middle of a gigantic hallway with a smooth marble floor. Orange-flamed torches lined the walls on both sides, providing just enough light to see from one end of the hallway to the other. Every square inch of the place seemed to be covered with strange carvings and decorations, and I found myself wondering if it was the prettiest place I'd ever been in or just the creepiest.

Gax kept the Torg moving one step at a time, each motion producing a soft echo.

"Where we goin', Gax?" Spuckler asked.

"I HAVEN'T THE FAINTEST IDEA, SIR," Gax replied. "I ASSUME WE HAVE TO KEEP MOVING, THOUGH, IF WE ARE TO AVOID AROUSING SUSPICION."

"Good thinking, Gax," said Mr. Beeba. "Still, we need to find some means of discerning the Prince's whereabouts. In a castle this size, it could take us months to search the place!"

Months? I didn't want to stay in that castle more than a few minutes! We'd *have* to find a better way.

Suddenly there was a warbly, gurgling sound: Poog was talking. It had been a while since I'd heard his alien language, so it caught me a bit off guard. We all turned and looked at Poog. He had a serious look on his face. The orange flames of the torches shimmered in his big

black eyes. He finished what he had to say, shut his mouth, and blinked once or twice.

"Poog says we've got to keep our eyes open," Mr. Beeba translated. "If we look carefully enough, we'll be able to see some sort of clue as to where the Prince is being held."

"Why doesn't he just *tell* us where he's bein' held," Spuckler grumbled, "'stead of being Mr. Mysterious all the time?"

"Hush, Spuckler," Mr. Beeba scolded. "It is not for us to decide what Poog will or will not tell us!"

"Yeah, yeah, yeah," Spuckler muttered, sounding as though he'd heard Mr. Beeba say this many times before.

So Gax kept the Torg going, and we all peered out of our dark little compartment into the dim orange light, hoping to see something cluelike. Once, another Torg came into view, heading to some other part of the castle. It made a short beeping sound as it passed, one that Gax was careful to repeat. I figured that was the way Torgs greeted one another, like people back in Middleton saying "Hi" as they passed on the street.

"This is crazy," Spuckler said after a few minutes. "We're not gonna get anywhere wanderin' around like this. I say we climb down an' check the place out on foot."

"Absolutely not," Mr. Beeba replied sternly. "This Torg is the only thing keeping us from being discovered!"

"Yeah," Spuckler protested. "But it's so *boring!*"

Suddenly I saw a tiny robot pass in front of us. It was about three feet tall and clattered across the floor like a vacuum cleaner with legs. It made three high-pitched beeps and continued on its way. I looked down and saw that it was carrying a tray in one of its mechanical hands. On the tray was . . . well, I know it sounds crazy, but I'd swear it looked exactly like *milk and cookies!*

Chapter 6

"**Gax,**" I **said** excitedly. "Follow that robot!"

"BUT, MA'AM—" Gax began.

"Just follow it!" I said again. "I'll bet *anything* that little guy's heading straight to the Prince!"

"Do what she says, Gax," Spuckler said, not sounding entirely sure why he was saying it. " 'Kiko's got her mind made up on this one."

So Gax made the Torg stop, pivot, and follow the miniature robot down a corridor that branched off from the main hallway. Gax left twenty-five or thirty feet between the two robots, evidently trying not to look too suspicious.

The corridor was darker and had fewer decorations on its walls than the grand hallway we'd just come from. The ceiling was also pretty low, leaving just enough space for the Torg to get through. It occurred to me that we were making rather a lot of noise walking down the hallway with our robot's enormous metal feet. Could the miniature robot hear us?

GREEEEEET!

As if it had heard my question, the little robot abruptly came to a stop and spun its head around to confront us. I couldn't tell if it looked angry or not (How could I? It didn't have any eyebrows!), but it didn't seem particularly happy to see us either.

"Keep goin', Gax!" Spuckler whispered. "He'll get suspicious if we stop!"

Gax obediently made the Torg walk right by the little robot as if we were on our way somewhere. The other robot's head slowly swiveled as we passed, its mechanical eyes locked on us.

"But, Spuckler," I whispered, "if we keep going like this, we're going to lose the trail!"

"Don't worry, 'Kiko. I got a plan."

Mr. Beeba whimpered quietly like a wounded dog. I think he tended to get really nervous whenever Spuckler had a plan.

Gax kept the Torg walking until we were forty-five or fifty feet ahead of the little robot. Then Spuckler spoke again.

"All right, Gax," he said, "stop here and act like you're workin' on the walls."

"WORKING ON THE WALLS, SIR?" Gax asked, sounding thoroughly mystified.

"Pretend you're waterproofin', or fixin' the caulk or something."

"THERE *IS* NO CAULK, SIR . . . ," said Gax.

Spuckler growled.

". . . BUT I'LL SEE WHAT I CAN DO," Gax added hastily.

With that he raised one of the Torg's arms and began urgently poking at a spot where the wall met the ceiling.

It was eerily quiet as Spuckler, Mr. Beeba, Poog, Gax, and I huddled together in the dark compartment, waiting to find out what would happen next. Mr. Beeba

pulled a handkerchief from under his belt and began patting his damp forehead.

Finally we heard the light skittering sound of the little robot's feet on the stone floor as it approached us from behind. Gax made several of the Torg's arms shoot out to fiddle even more vigorously with various areas of the wall, producing an impressive variety of noises. It sounded like a whole team of construction workers using everything from jackhammers to power drills. I don't know whether Gax really had any idea what he was supposed to be doing, but he was definitely making the Torg look *busy*.

NIRKLE-NIRKLE GLEEP-GLEEP!

The little robot passed us and continued down the corridor, its tray of milk and cookies held proudly before it in two mechanical fists.

"Wh-what did he say?" Mr. Beeba asked, mopping his forehead.

"HE TOLD ME I MISSED A SPOT."

Chapter 7

Gax continued to follow the little robot, stopping periodically to "work" a bit on the walls. Eventually we came to a point where the corridor opened into a large rectangular room with one smallish square door at the far end. Two large lizardy-looking animals with shiny gray-green skin and pointy yellow teeth were guarding the door, one chained at either side. When the robot arrived, they jumped up and yanked against their chains, growling and snapping at the air like rabid pit bulls.

"Vungers," Spuckler whispered to me. "They're snow lizards. Pretty fierce little critters. They could eat a guy like Beebs for breakfast an' still have room for pancakes."

Mr. Beeba shot Spuckler an annoyed glance and raised his head for a better view.

TWEEEEEEEEEEEEEP!

The little robot emitted a piercing whistle so high-pitched I could barely hear it. My skin broke out in goose pimples, and a weird shiver ran up and down my spine. The two lizards suddenly lay down with their jaws on the floor, closed their beady black eyes, and fell fast asleep.

The little robot inserted a small key into a keyhole on the right-hand side of the door and gave it series of turns.

KAK! P'CHIK! KREEEEEEE . . .

The robot opened the door, closing it quickly behind itself after entering the room. A few seconds passed before the door opened again and the robot reemerged, this time without the tray of food.

"Gax!" Spuckler growled. "Work, buddy, *work!*"

Gax quickly resumed his fixing-the-walls routine, turning the entire Torg toward the wall as if it had just discovered a particularly troublesome spot. The little robot beeped loudly as it passed and clattered back down the hallway, eyeing us suspiciously as it disappeared from view.

"The Prince is in that room!" I said, pushing the hatch up with both hands and rising to my feet. "I *know* it!"

"I hope you're right, Akiko," Mr. Beeba said, tucking his handkerchief back under his belt. "It would make this whole rescuing business *ever* so much easier."

Spuckler disconnected the cable linking Gax to the head of the Torg, then stopped, seeming to think better of it.

"You better stay here with th' Torg, ol' buddy," he explained as he reconnected the thick metallic cord. "We might need t' make a speedy getaway or somethin', ya know what I mean?"

"CERTAINLY, SIR," Gax answered, sounding as if he feared our getaway would be anything but speedy.

"Atta boy," said Spuckler.

I helped Mr. Beeba lower himself to the floor, then jumped down to join him. Spuckler and Poog followed, and we all tiptoed carefully across the room, trying our best not to awaken the snoozing Vungers. A troubled silence fell over us as we stared at the solid-looking door. Spuckler tried turning the knob. It wouldn't budge.

"We could try picking the lock," I suggested, even though I didn't know the first thing about lock picking. I'd seen my uncle Koji do it once back in Middleton, but I had no idea *how* he did it.

"Pickin' locks is for sissies," said Spuckler as he strutted back to the Torg and began climbing up to the storage compartment. "I got a better idea."

Mr. Beeba gave me a nervous glance. He looked as if he might need his handkerchief again soon.

"Spuckler!" I called as loudly as I could without waking the Vungers. "What, um, *sort* of idea do you have in mind?"

"You'll see!" he replied cheerfully.

Every once in a while he'd pop up out of the Torg's head to examine some tool in the torchlight, then toss it back in and dive down for another look.

"That ain't it. . . . Naw, this ain't it neither. . . ."

"Really now, Spuckler,"
Mr. Beeba whispered angrily.
"I *insist* that you tell us what
you're up to."

"Got it!" Spuckler
announced, proudly
holding a small metallic
box in one hand. He
leaped from the top of
the Torg to the floor in a
single bound and trotted

quickly over to the square door.

I glanced at Poog. He had a slightly troubled look on
his face.

"Um, Spuckler," I whispered, "what *is* that thing?"

"Well, 'Kiko, that all depends on whatcher *usin'* it
for," he answered as he attached the little box to a spot
on the door just below the keyhole. "Today it's whatcha
might call an automatic door opener—"

"Spuckler!" Mr. Beeba interrupted. "I don't like the
sound of this one little bit! I demand—I say, I *demand*
you tell us what you're planning to do!"

Spuckler pulled a little pin out of the box and stood up.

"Stan' back, everybody," he said, leading us all away from the door to a spot just behind the Torg. "We only got about ten seconds. Or was it five?"

We all watched the door. Mr. Beeba, perhaps already knowing what was about to happen, turned away and clamped his hands firmly over the sides of his head.

Chik-chik-chik . . .

KA-BLOOOOOOOOOOOOOOOM!!!

There was a tremendous flash of light. A whizzing, whistling noise filled the air as something—probably the doorknob—shot by us and ricocheted down the hall. Within seconds the entire room was choked with great clouds of black smoke. My ears were still ringing with the sound of the explosion when I realized I could also hear the Vungers. And they weren't snoring, either.

Chapter 8

"You idiot!" Mr. Beeba cried.

"Got the door open, didn' I?" Spuckler replied, admiring his own handiwork.

Sure enough, there was now practically nothing *left* of the door but a few scraps of wood near the bottom left side. It would be no trouble for all of us to just walk right in . . .

. . . except for the Vungers.

They were growling and snapping and lunging at us with all their might, their long lizardy tails whipping this way and that, bits of saliva flying from their mouths every time they moved.

"You *idiot!*" Mr. Beeba repeated. "We'll *never* get in there now!"

"Sure we will," Spuckler replied nonchalantly. "We'll jus' have to run *real* fast."

"R-r-run?" Mr. Beeba asked through clenched teeth, his eyes nearly popping out of his head. "We couldn't get past those beasts if we ran a hundred miles per *hour!*"

"We could, uh, get back inside the Torg . . . ," Spuckler muttered, staring doubtfully at the enormous robot, ". . . and, um, try an' *squeeze* through. . . ."

I looked at the Torg and compared its size to that of the doorway. Any fool could see we'd never get such a large robot through such a small space. I looked at Poog, hoping he might have an idea. He stared blankly back, as if the matter were entirely up to me. Meanwhile the Vungers began howling and yelping like starving wolves. We had to act fast; sooner or later someone was bound to hear them and come to check things out.

Suddenly it hit me.

"Gax," I called.

"YES, MA'AM?" he replied, poking his squarish little head out of the Torg's storage compartment to look at me.

"Did you hear that little robot's whistle?" I asked. "The one that made the Vungers go to sleep?"

Spuckler looked at me with his big round eyes, a smile of understanding forming on his lips.

"I COULD HARDLY HAVE FAILED TO HEAR IT, MA'AM," Gax answered. "IT WAS EXCESSIVELY LOUD. A VERY HIGH G-SHARP, I BELIEVE."

By this time everyone was looking at Gax, Poog included.

"Can you imitate that sound?" I asked.

"I . . . ," said Gax uncertainly, seeming to grow nervous with so many eyes fixed upon him. "I COULD CERTAINLY TRY, MA'AM."

"Well, go on, buddy," Spuckler cried. "We ain't got all day!"

Gax stuck his neck out of the storage compartment as far as he could. There was a low grinding sound, almost as if he were clearing his mechanical throat.

BLEEEEET!

We all stared hopefully at the Vungers, who continued yelping and clawing at the floor with wild abandon, looking, if anything, even *more* ferocious than before.

"PERHAPS I WAS A BIT FLAT," said Gax apologetically.

We all held our tongues as Gax prepared for another try. Mr. Beeba, in particular, looked as though he was about to faint with anxiety.

Gax raised his head as far as his scrawny little neck could reach and made another low grinding sound, this time quivering a bit and rocking ever so slightly from side to side.

TWEEEET!

Suddenly one of the Vungers leaped forward so violently it actually snapped its chain and hurled itself across the room. It tumbled comically across the floor before getting to its feet and confronting all of us from a mere three or four feet away, its enormous body neatly blocking the hallway. It was now cutting off our only means of escape.

Mr. Beeba's teeth began to chatter uncontrollably, and even Spuckler looked a little unsure of what to do next. I backed up until I was flat against the wall behind me. There was nowhere left to run.

TWEEEEEEEEEEEEP!

The Vungers each gave one last yelp before collapsing to the floor. Within seconds they were sound asleep, one still chained to the side of the door, the other just inches from Spuckler's feet.

"All *right!*" I cried, reflexively undoing the buttons of my thick warm coat. I was sweating all over.

"Good goin', Gax!" Spuckler cheered. "Try t' remember that sound, now. Ya never know when it's gonna come in handy."

"Very finely executed, my rusty-headed friend," said

Mr. Beeba. "I never doubted you for an instant." (If you ask me, he'd never *stopped* doubting anyone in his entire *life*.)

"Who *is* that out there?" came a small voice from the other side of the doorway.

Spuckler and Mr. Beeba shot each other a knowing glance. Poog stared intently at me, the slightest trace of a smile on his face.

"That's him!" said Mr. Beeba. *"Prince Froptoppit!"*

Chapter 9

One by one we tiptoed through the charred remains of the doorway. The room was small and slightly damp, with just one weakly flickering torch on the wall. I saw a simple bed, a wooden table and chair, and a large chest of drawers. And there, sitting on the floor with his back against the wall, was Prince Froptoppit.

He looked about eight years old. He was covered from head to toe in a clean white suit of clothes, with silvery bands on his arms, a large round cap on his head, and a short white cape hanging from his shoulders to the middle of his back. He had big brown eyes, pale pink cheeks, and longish black hair that was neatly cropped just above his shoulders. He was kind of cute, actually, in his own way. But he looked slightly dazed.

"Mr. Beeba?" he asked, an excited smile spreading across his face. "Poog?"

"Relax, dear boy!" Mr. Beeba said, rushing to his side. "Don't get up just yet. I can see you've been through no end of trauma these last few weeks."

"Man oh man," Spuckler said, dropping down on one knee. "You are a sight for sore eyes, Prince Froptoppit. You got no idea what we been through t' get here."

The Prince turned his attention to me.

"Wh-who are *you*?"

"This is Akiko, Your Highness," Mr. Beeba explained, raising an opened hand in my direction. "She's from the planet Earth."

"A Keego?" said Prince Froptoppit, trying his best to pronounce my name.

"It's an honor to finally meet you, Prince Froptoppit," I said, hardly believing that I'd finally come face to face with him after all this time. He was smaller and less princely-looking than I'd pictured him, but believe

me, I've never been so happy to meet someone in my entire life.

"D-do you want some cookies?" he asked, turning to look at the empty tray beside him. "Uh-oh," he added, looking a little embarrassed. "I already ate them all."

"Well, at least they've been feeding you," Mr. Beeba said, picking up the empty glass from the tray and sniffing it suspiciously. "Hopefully more than just cookies!"

"Yes, Mr. Beeba," Prince Froptoppit replied. "I get all the food I need. I'm awfully lonely, though. I miss my father."

"And he misses *you*, Prince Froptoppit, more than words can say!" Mr. Beeba said, helping the Prince to his feet. "Come on. We're getting you out of here. Right *now*."

With that Spuckler swept the Prince into his arms and carried him out of the room. The rest of us followed, walking gingerly past the sleeping Vungers, which—thank goodness—snored loudly and steadily the whole time.

My head was crawling with questions. I swallowed

hard and determined to save them until we'd gotten out of the castle. There would be plenty of time for sorting things out once we'd escaped.

"This is almos' too *easy*," Spuckler said as he carried the Prince to the top of the Torg. "Now if we can jus' clear on outta here before anyone catches on . . ."

After we had everyone settled in (it took a bit of rearranging to make space for the Prince), Spuckler lowered the hatch and ordered Gax to go back to the main hallway. Prince Froptoppit leaned his head against my shoulder. I think it had been a long, long time since he'd been surrounded by friends. Gax made the Torg move forward as we carefully retraced our steps out of the castle.

Spuckler was right. It *was* almost too easy.

A moment later we were back in the big hallway, making our way toward the main entrance. My heart was pounding. Another twenty yards or so and we'd be free. I had a very vivid picture in my mind of King Froptoppit shaking my hand after we'd returned to the palace.

"You see, Akiko?" I imagined him saying with a big

toothy smile. "I *told* you you were the perfect person for this job!"

Ten more yards to the gate. I thought there would be another robot camera thing asking us questions before we left, but it was actually much simpler to leave the castle than to get in. By merely approaching the door we somehow triggered it to open, just like an automatic door at the supermarket. We all peered out excitedly as the enormous gate began to rise, piercing the air with a rusty screeching. I had to squint as my eyes readjusted to the bright light of the outdoors. Gax made the Torg take the last few steps out into the snow, then suddenly stopped.

"I *knew* it," said Spuckler.

My heart sank as I looked out the half-open hatch. It was Throck. He was standing there waiting for us.

Chapter 10

HHSSSSSSSSHHH!

He stood with his arms folded, his powerful legs ankle-deep in the snow, his black-and-gray armor every so often sending a great cloud of steam up into the pale sunlight. Behind him were more than a dozen Torgs, spread out like a battalion of tanks.

They were armed with all sorts of guns and missiles and stuff, and every last piece of their weaponry was aimed directly at us.

HHSSSSSSSSHHH!

Another cloud of exhaust rose from behind Throck's head as he savored his moment of victory. His short-cropped hair was nearly as white as the mountain peaks above him. His scar-ravaged face was scrunched up in an expression of disdain.

"Leaving so soon?" he sneered. "Rather impolite of you, don't you think?"

Spuckler opened the hatch and rose to his feet. Mr. Beeba gasped hoarsely and crouched farther down on the floor of the compartment.

"Out of our way, Throck," Spuckler shouted without the slightest trace of fear. "We got the Prince, and we're takin' him back home where he belongs!"

HHSSSSSSSSHHH!

Throck squinted and clenched his teeth.

"You're going *nowhere!*" he growled.

Raising one hand in the air, Throck ordered the group of Torgs to open fire on us.

With lightning-fast reflexes, Spuckler pulled the hatch firmly shut. A split second later our Torg began rocking from side to side under a barrage of laser fire. With the hatch closed the compartment was pitch-black. The noise of laser blasts grew louder and louder, and our Torg shook violently under the strain. We were thrown first in one direction, then another, before finally whirling around and slamming to the ground.

Throck barked an order and the shooting stopped.

I lay there in the darkness almost unable to breathe. The compartment filled with oily-smelling fumes. I could feel the Prince's face pushed up against me on one side. Mr. Beeba's oversized feet jabbed into my ribs on the other.

T- T-K'CHAK!

Throck pried the hatch open and we all tumbled out into the snow. Encircled by Torgs, their weapons still smoking from the attack, we huddled together on our knees in the hazy midday light. The Prince, now wide awake, quivered and curled up next to me like a small frightened animal. Only Poog seemed unconcerned by this latest turn of events. He floated proudly above us, staring at Throck with an expression of unshakable determination.

HHSSSSSSSSHHH!

"I've got to hand it to you people," Throck muttered, carefully directing his gaze away from Poog. "Your persistence knows no bounds."

He began slowly walking around us with his hands tucked behind him, circling again and again like a prowling tiger.

"You scaled the Great Wall of Trudd. . . . You marched for hours through slush and snow. . . . You even had the *audacity* to enter this castle uninvited," he said, shaking his head in disbelief. "You'll do *anything* to rescue this dear little boy, won't you?"

"That's right! We will!" I heard myself say, startled to realize that I was now standing up and pointing my finger right in Throck's face. "And that includes putting *you* behind bars!"

Mr. Beeba and Spuckler looked at me with popped-out eyes and wide-open mouths. I think I'd succeeded in shocking everyone else as much as I'd shocked myself. My heart was beating at incredible speed, and I could feel the blood rushing to my face. There was a weird tingly feeling all over my body, as if I were surrounded by a warm cloak of electricity.

Throck stopped and turned to face me, looking half amused, half genuinely surprised.

"You've got a lot of nerve, little girl," he said after a long silence. "I'm *impressed*. It's a shame old Froptoppit got hold of you before *I* did—"

"If you know what's good for you," I interrupted, still pointing my finger directly at Throck's eyes, "you'll let us go."

Throck stared at me so intently that it

almost seemed as if he *would* let us go. He had a very distant look in his eyes, which gradually turned into an almost *kindly* look. I could nearly imagine that he was quietly smiling behind that black breathing mask of his.

"Children," he whispered, seeming to stare *at* me and *through* me at the same time. "They have such a simple way of looking at things."

He paused, the kindly look in his eyes slowly twisting itself into a menacing scowl.

"Isn't it a shame they all have to grow up and see how *messy* life really is?"

"You heard the girl, Throck," Spuckler said, rising to stand right beside me. "Call off your little goon squad here, and then maybe we'll decide to let you go."

"You," said Throck, his beady little eyes flying open wide, "will let *me* go?" He tossed his head back and let out a loud cackling laugh that echoed repeatedly off the surrounding mountain walls. Gax rattled uncontrollably, Mr. Beeba moaned, and the Prince scooted as close to me as he possibly could.

"Perhaps I need to clarify the situation for you,"

Throck said, glaring at Spuckler with renewed fury, the volume of his voice growing with every word. "The only reason you are still alive at this moment is because I have *allowed* it to be so! I could do away with the *lot* of you right now if I wanted to, and no one would even—"

Suddenly Throck stopped himself and stepped back, as if he were afraid he'd crossed some invisible line. He took one or two more steps back and stood motionless in the snow, a strangely tense expression on his face.

It was Poog.

Poog had risen, moved past Spuckler's shoulder, and was now floating forward, slowly and steadily moving in a straight line toward Throck's face. He came to a stop just a few inches away from the bridge of Throck's nose. From where I was sitting I couldn't see Poog's face. I can only imagine his expression at that moment.

Throck was terrified. I could see it in his eyes. His forehead was creased with a maze of deep wrinkles. A single drop of sweat rolled down one side of his face and fell noiselessly into the snow. I'll bet he'd never been so scared before in his entire life. Still, he seemed determined not to back down.

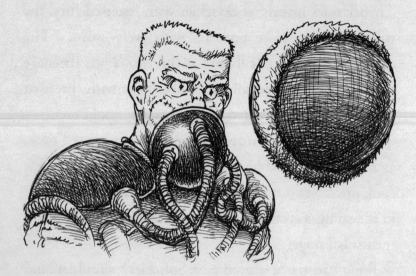

Poog said something to Throck in a strange language I'd never heard him use before. It was very different from his usual high-pitched warble. This was a deep, throaty sound that rose and fell between two precise notes, like the chanting of monks in some spooky alien monastery.

There was a long pause. Throck appeared to be considering what Poog had said to him. Then he answered, replying in the very same language, but with many more pauses and muttering sounds, as if he were far less sure of what he wanted to say than Poog was.

"Beebs," I heard Spuckler whisper, "you catchin' any of this?"

"Not a word," Mr. Beeba answered. "It's a language I've never encountered before. But it seems to me that they're"—he paused, searching for the right word—"*negotiating.*"

Every once in a while Throck would raise his voice, slicing his hands through the air in frustration. Poog kept calm, answering Throck's outbursts with brief, measured sentences, never even pausing to collect his thoughts. After ten or fifteen minutes of going back and forth like this, they finally seemed to come to some sort of agreement. Poog turned and floated back to join us, his face expressionless, businesslike. Throck cleared his throat to speak.

"You will be granted an audience with Alia Rellapor," he announced, sounding considerably less imposing than he had only a few moments before. "She will decide what is to be done with you.

"But make no mistake," he added, staring directly at me. "You will *not* be permitted to take the Prince from this castle."

chapter 11

Throck led us back into the castle and down the vast main hallway. There were a bunch of Torgs in front of us and even more following behind. He led us up grand marble staircases and across great cavernous rooms with ceilings hundreds of feet high. He ushered us through many gateways, each one more spectacular than the last. It seemed we were being led to the very heart of the castle.

I wrapped my arms around myself as I walked along with the others, wondering what it would be like to finally meet Alia Rellapor face to face. Would she be as scary-looking as Throck? Would she be even *scarier*? Would she punish us for attempting to rescue the Prince?

The more questions I came up with, the less I really wanted to know the answers. Just then I pictured myself back in my bedroom. It had been so long since I'd even *thought* about home. The sudden vivid picture in my mind took me completely by surprise. I saw myself lying belly-down on the floor, my head resting on one hand, the other hand flipping lazily through a magazine. One of my favorite songs was playing on the radio. The sun was pouring in through the window, and the smell of my mom's cooking was floating up from the kitchen. . . .

I'd have given anything to be back there. Anything at all. I hate to say it, but I'd have said goodbye to everyone—Spuckler, Mr. Beeba, Poog, *everyone*—and just never looked back. I was so tired and cold and hungry, I just didn't care about anything anymore. I stared gloomily at the gray polished-stone floor and kept walking.

Throck and his robot troops eventually took us into a large room with dark stone walls. At one end there was an enormous blackish-red curtain that stretched from floor to ceiling and wall to wall, preventing us from seeing even a glimpse of what lay beyond it. The room was lit by small flickering torches on the walls, held behind transparent domes of red-tinted glass. Against one wall stood a long wooden bench. Throck instructed us to sit down and wait. The Torgs formed a row on the other side of the room, their weaponry still

carefully trained on us. Throck then disappeared behind the thick red curtain and left us there in a silence that was interrupted only by the low, steady buzzing of the Torgs.

Whatever Throck was doing, it was taking him a long time. I glanced around and saw that everyone was looking more dejected than they had during the entire mission. Mr. Beeba had his head in his hands and was staring at his feet with an expression of utter despair. Spuckler was twiddling his thumbs and staring bitterly at the Torgs across the room. Gax was rocking very slowly from side to side, and the Prince had a strange glassy look in his eyes, as if he were wishing that he could be magically whisked off to his own sunny room somewhere. Only Poog remained unfazed. He looked very strong and stoic, as if he were preparing himself for something he'd seen coming for a very long time.

I decided to start a conversation, thinking it might take everyone's minds off the misery of our current circumstances. Well, it was worth a try, anyway.

"Prince Froptoppit," I asked, "how was it that you

got kidnapped? Did Alia Rellapor break into your bed-room and capture you or something?"

"No . . . uh, not exactly," the Prince replied hesitantly. "I was out in the palace gardens. Have you ever seen the palace gardens, Akiko?"

"No," I answered. "I never got the chance."

"That's a shame," said the Prince. "They're really lovely. There are flowers there from nearly every planet in the galaxy——"

"So, um," I interrupted, "Alia Rellapor just sort of swooped down into the gardens and kidnapped you? Is that how it happened?"

"Uh . . . ," said the Prince, looking extremely uncomfortable, ". . . yeah. More or less."

There was a long pause. I glanced at Spuckler and Mr. Beeba. Each of them shifted his gaze elsewhere. I had a very strange feeling that I'd just started a conversation no one particularly wanted to have. Which for some reason just made me all the more anxious to have it.

"So why does Alia Rellapor hate your father so

much, Prince Froptoppit?" I asked. "What did he ever do to her?"

The Prince stared at me with an expression of extreme agitation. He glanced pointedly at Mr. Beeba and Spuckler, as if my questions were signs that they had failed to explain something to me—something very, very important. Mr. Beeba and Spuckler looked taken aback.

"Come on," I said, now feeling extremely anxious to get some decent answers. "It's a simple enough question. What is Alia Rellapor's problem with King Froptoppit?"

"Well . . . ," the Prince began, now looking directly at Mr. Beeba, as if waiting for permission.

"This red-tinted torchlight is *really* unpleasant, don't you think?" Mr. Beeba asked, trying to sound casual and failing miserably at it. "I should think a nice warm shade of yellow would have shown this room off to *much* better effect. . . ."

"Yeah, Beebs," Spuckler added loudly, sounding even more unnatural than Mr. Beeba had. "Warm yellow. You're, uh, right on the money there—"

"What's going on here?" I interrupted. "Why are you two trying to change the subject?"

"Wh-who's trying to ch-change the subject?" Mr. Beeba stammered.

"*You're* trying to change the subject," I said. "And you're doing a pretty lousy job of it too."

"I . . . ," Mr. Beeba gasped, his eyes darting around and doing everything but meeting my gaze, "I'm sure I don't know *what* you're talking about, Akiko."

"You're hiding something from me, aren't you?" I asked.

"Hiding something?" Spuckler and Mr. Beeba said in unison. They looked so uptight I could have popped them both like balloons.

"There's something you're trying to keep me from finding out," I said angrily. "Something about Alia Rellapor."

"No, no, *no*, Akiko," Mr. Beeba protested, his eyes finally looking directly into mine. "I mean . . . ," he continued, swallowing hard and seeming almost to shrink a little right there in front of me, ". . . yes."

Chapter 12

"I knew it!" I cried, jumping to my feet, my voice sounding much louder than I intended. "You've been *lying* to me! I can't believe this!"

I was shivering like crazy. I felt hot and cold at the same time. It seemed as if everything I'd been depending on for the past five days was suddenly collapsing and falling apart.

" 'Kiko, 'Kiko!" Spuckler said, rising to grab me by the shoulders. "Calm down, now, it ain't like that. We would never lie to you jus' to be mean," he added, a sad and apologetic look in his eyes. "We were under *orders.*"

"Orders?" I asked, tears welling up in my eyes. "Whose orders?"

"My father's," answered a quiet voice. It was Prince Froptoppit. He was staring gravely at Spuckler and Mr. Beeba, suddenly looking much older than his years. "He ordered you not to tell her, didn't he?"

They both nodded solemnly. My heart sank and my stomach felt very tight and slightly queasy. I turned to look at Poog. He had a calm, resigned look in his eyes, as if something he'd known was unavoidable was finally coming to pass.

"He ordered you not to tell me *what*?" I asked, choking back tears.

The heavy red curtain flew open and Throck stepped back into the room, his polished armor gleaming in the red glow of the torches. The Torgs whirred and buzzed some sort of electronic salute. Throck turned to face us.

"Rise!" he said gruffly. "Empress Rellapor will see you now."

"*Empress?*" Spuckler sneered. "Pretty ambitious, ain't she?"

"Oh yes, little man," Throck answered, a strangely

happy gleam in his eyes. "She is ambitious in ways you can barely comprehend."

My head was spinning. I still couldn't believe that Mr. Beeba and Spuckler were hiding something from me. I thought they were my *friends*. And now we were being taken to meet Alia Rellapor, at the very moment I felt least prepared to face her. What would she look like? What would she *be* like?

The Torgs stepped forward, parted the curtains, and held them back so that we could all pass through. Throck went first, followed by Spuckler and Gax, then by the Prince and me, and finally by Mr. Beeba and Poog. We stepped one by one into a room that was much larger but even more poorly lit than the one we'd just been in. The floor was a vast sheet of polished stone. The walls were covered with ornate decorations. The ceiling, somewhere high above, was hidden in shadows. At the far end of the room stood a large throne of gold lit by a semicircle of enormous candles.

Sitting on the throne was a small woman dressed in a simple gray cloak. As we walked across the floor to where she sat, her dimly lit features became clearer and

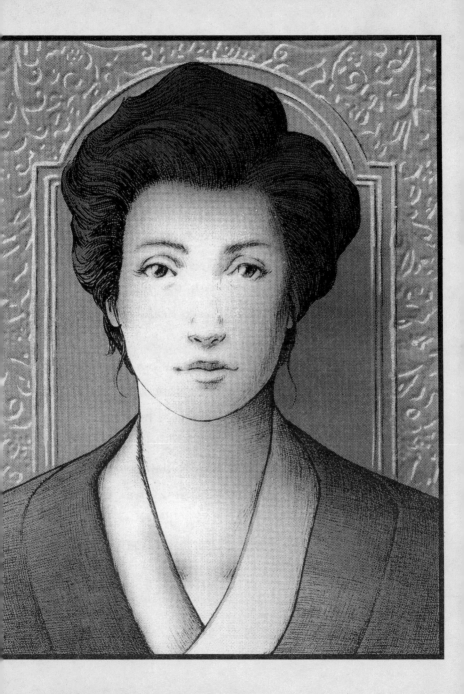

clearer. She had jet-black hair pulled back loosely from her face, with one or two curls hanging down at her neck. Her eyes were deep brown and very kind looking, her nose narrow and elegant. Her rose-colored lips were drawn ever so slightly back into a gentle smile.

She was one of the most beautiful women I'd ever seen. She looked like an ancient Greek goddess. Surely this wasn't Alia Rellapor. There must be some mistake.

"Don't worry, friends," she said to us, her voice soft and clear. "I won't gobble you up like some sort of monster, though the tales you've heard about me may have led you to expect as much."

I glanced quickly at the others. Spuckler and Mr. Beeba both looked somewhat stunned, as if they had forgotten how beautiful Alia was. The Prince looked both frightened and, somehow, slightly excited. Poog's expression was blank, as if Alia Rellapor were not even there before him. But strangest of all was Throck. He looked scrunched up and tense, like a man playing a tremendously important chess game. Perhaps he, too, was uncomfortable in the presence of Alia Rellapor?

As for me, I must have looked a little starstruck. Alia

Rellapor was so much lovelier than I had imagined her to be!

"Now tell me," she said with a smile. "Which of you is the leader of this little group?"

There was a long pause. Mr. Beeba elbowed me sharply in the ribs.

"I am," I said, lurching forward awkwardly. "M-my name is Akiko."

"You're a very brave girl, Akiko," she said, "and clever, too. Leading this group past so many obstacles, and for so many miles, doing without proper food or a roof over your head . . . It's all very impressive. I could use a girl like you on my side. You should

forget about old King Froptoppit and just stay here with me."

She spoke so naturally and sweetly that part of me actually wanted to be on her side. Was this what they hadn't told me about Alia Rellapor? That she was a very nice person, that her horrible reputation was undeserved?

"But . . . ," I said, my voice quivering, unsure of how to reply, ". . . but I can't stay here with you. I'm here to rescue the Prince."

"Rescue?" she repeated with an astonished smile. "Is that what King Froptoppit told you? That the Prince needed rescuing? You have been lied to, Akiko."

"Come here," she said, turning to Prince Froptoppit. "Come and stand beside me."

The Prince stepped forward, hesitantly at first, his eyes searching Alia Rellapor as if he were not quite sure of his own feelings toward her. Finally, though, he walked quickly to her side and put his hand in hers.

"How could I have kidnapped the Prince?" Alia Rellapor asked, stroking his hand gently with her own. "A mother cannot kidnap her own son."

Chapter 13

It was silent. The room was still. But inside me the whole world seemed to be caving in, swallowing me up into a black fog.

Her son? Her *son*? How could Prince Froptoppit be Alia Rellapor's son? It was impossible. Or was it? I felt so terribly dizzy all of a sudden, I didn't know *what* to think. With what little energy I had left, I stared intently at Prince Froptoppit, hoping to see some sign that this was all a dirty trick, that Alia Rellapor was no more related to him than I was. But I saw no such sign. The Prince leaned toward Alia Rellapor, allowing her to pull him onto her lap. He dropped his head onto her shoulder and closed his eyes peacefully. There could be no doubt about it. Alia Rellapor *was* the Prince's mother, and King Froptoppit—for *some* reason—had ordered Mr. Beeba and Spuckler not to tell me about it.

"So you see, Akiko," Alia Rellapor said with a smile, "King Froptoppit has deceived you. The Prince is here where he belongs. If you don't believe me, I invite you to return to your dear King and ask him to explain his lies to you. I'm sure he will have invented some very interesting explanations by now. . . ."

"But—" I began. Something had just occurred to me, something that didn't fit.

"But what, dear child?"

"But if you're the Prince's mother," I went on, "then why are you keeping him locked up in a dirty little room? Why aren't you treating him better?"

For the first time Alia Rellapor's peacefully smiling face went blank. She looked stunned and terribly confused. Her mouth opened but no words came out.

Throck let out a strange sort of cough, like a man who'd been underwater coming up for air. His eyes remained unwaveringly focused on Alia Rellapor, though.

"Maybe King Froptoppit hasn't been completely truthful," I continued, "but one thing's for sure. He'd never keep the Prince locked up in a room like that. If you really *were* the Prince's mother, you wouldn't have to act like he's a prisoner."

"I will treat my son as I see fit!" she snapped, an angry frown sweeping over her face, her beautiful features suddenly not so beautiful anymore. The Prince's eyes fluttered open. He tried to move, but Alia held him fast with one arm.

"Why . . . ," I began, unsure of how she would react to another question.

Alia relaxed her face into a smile. Throck exhaled noisily through his breathing apparatus.

"Please, Akiko," she said. "Ask me any question you like."

"Why are you so angry at King Froptoppit?" I asked. "What did he do to make you want to hurt him so badly?"

Again Alia's face went blank. This time, though, she regained her self-control quickly and answered my question in a calm, quiet voice.

"I cannot abide King Froptoppit," she said, "because he is weak. He lacks the strength to run this planet properly."

Mr. Beeba's face tightened indignantly, but he held his tongue. Spuckler squinted suspiciously at Alia, but he also remained silent.

"The people of Smoo need a strong hand to guide them," she continued, her voice sounding harder, colder. "They need a ruler who won't hesitate to use harsh discipline whenever necessary. Just as the Prince needs a mother who refuses to pamper him with luxury and doting servants. The people of Smoo," she added, "need a ruler like *me*."

I shot another glance at Throck. This time he pivoted his head to meet my gaze, a triumphant look in his eyes. A single droplet of sweat ran down his forehead and fell off his cheek. I swallowed hard and turned back to Alia Rellapor.

"Couldn't you, um, talk this over with King Froptoppit?" I asked. "I'm sure he'd understand if you told him how you feel."

"No!" she answered, raising her voice angrily. "I will

not allow myself to be further contaminated by that cowardly little man!"

"But King Froptoppit's not so bad," I replied. "He—"

"Froptoppit is a fool!" she bellowed.

Her voice echoed loudly around the room. Mr. Beeba leaped back, quivering pathetically in Spuckler's shadow. Gax's spindly little neck was extended as far as it would go, his mechanical eyes opened wide. Prince Froptoppit tensed but dared not move. Even Throck looked a little  startled, but also pleased, as if he thoroughly approved of Alia's performance. Only Poog remained unimpressed, his face as blank as it had been when we first entered the room.

"The King and his ilk will not survive, I tell you," Alia continued, her voice trembling with anger, her pretty face twisted into an ugly scowl. "It is the natural order of things that weak rulers be cast aside by strong ones."

There was a pause as Alia allowed the full implication of her words to sink in.

"So make your choice now, Akiko," she added, staring into my eyes, "for when I seize power, I will show no mercy to Froptoppit and his deluded followers. I will uproot them like weeds, I will exterminate them like the pests they are!"

The gentle, kind Alia Rellapor of a moment before had utterly disappeared, replaced by a woman every bit as frightening as Throck himself.

"But—" I began.

"Enough!" Alia snapped. "I am weary of this fruitless conversation. You have trespassed upon my property. You have attempted to steal my son away from me. You must be punished."

She turned to face Throck, who watched her every move with great concentration.

"Tell me, my friend," Alia said, "what would you say to the idea of putting these intruders into the hole?"

"An excellent choice, Empress Rellapor," Throck answered, sounding slightly winded.

"Very well, then," Alia said. "Escort them there at once. We'll see if they won't reconsider their loyalty to old Froptoppit."

A half dozen Torgs emerged from the shadows, encircling us like a snare. Spuckler looked as though he wanted to fight them but for once could see that this was a battle he could not win. Throck raised an arm, barked a few orders, and led us, Torgs and all, back out of the room.

I turned around and caught one last glimpse of the Prince as we left. He still sat there on Alia Rellapor's lap, his face anxious, his body looking too tired to move. I wondered if it was the last I'd ever see of him. I certainly *hoped* it was the last I'd see of Alia Rellapor.

Before long we were being herded through a dark, damp corridor that felt like the passageway to a medieval dungeon. As we moved farther and farther into the blackness, I tried to make sense of some of the

things I'd just seen and heard. It wasn't easy. The thought that Alia Rellapor was the Prince's mother was so devastating I didn't want to face it, and the idea that King Froptoppit and Mr. Beeba and everybody had been lying to me was enough to make me sick. My head was spinning with so many questions, I didn't know who was lying and who was telling the truth. Why did Alia Rellapor seem so nice at first and then turn so nasty? Did she really hate King Froptoppit simply because he was weak, or was that just some excuse? Why hadn't Poog said anything on our behalf the way he had before?

As for the hole, well, I didn't even want to *think* about what that might turn out to be.

Chapter 14

After we had passed through the long, dark hallway, Throck led us into a huge round room. In the middle of the floor we saw a pit that must have been twenty feet wide. Above the pit, hanging from a sooty black chain, was a large iron cage with a single squarish door. On one side of the pit, a narrow stone platform jutted out to meet the bottom of the door to the cage. Throck stepped across the platform, opened the cage door with a loud, rattling screech, and walked back to where we stood at the edge of the hole.

"You!" he barked, grabbing Spuckler roughly by one arm. "Into the cage!"

Spuckler stood fast where he was.

"Make me," he said through gritted teeth.

"With pleasure," Throck answered, snapping his gigantic hand around Spuckler's neck. Spuckler gave a muffled cry as Throck lifted him and carried him toward the pit like a fisherman lugging his latest catch. All at once he tossed Spuckler violently into the cage, which creaked and swayed with the added weight.

"Now," Throck said, turning to face us. "I trust I can expect a bit more cooperation from the rest of you."

"Absolutely, er, Mr. Throck, sir," Mr. Beeba squeaked as he obediently trotted into the cage. "Come now, Akiko," he called back to me as he sat down by Spuckler's side. "We mustn't keep Mr. Throck waiting. You can see he's a very *busy* man."

I shot Throck an angry glance as I followed Mr. Beeba into the cage. Staring down into the pit as I stepped across the platform, I shuddered at its depth. The bottom—if there *was* a bottom—was completely engulfed in blackness.

Gax followed me, rolling carefully over the gap between the cage and the edge of the platform. Only Poog remained, confronting Throck directly for the first time since they had "negotiated" outside the castle.

A tense, silent moment passed. I thought for sure Poog would say or do something to save us. But he simply stared at Throck. Finally, without a word, Poog floated over the platform and joined us inside the cage. Throck leaped forward and locked the door of the cage as quickly as he could. He seemed to breathe a sigh of relief.

"I told you you'd never leave this castle with the

Prince," said Throck. He turned and walked to a long iron lever on the wall. "Now it looks like you'll never leave this castle *at all.*"

He reached up and swiftly pulled the lever all the way down. Immediately the cage dropped a few inches, stopped abruptly, then slowly continued to descend into the pit.

KUK-KUK-KUK-KUK-KUK-
KUK-KUK-KUK-KUK-KUK . . .

As the chain lowered the cage, there was a horrible rusty cranking sound, like the noise of a monstrous roller coaster carrying thrill seekers to the top of its highest hill. I caught one last glimpse of Throck as we dropped below the edge of the hole. He had his arms folded across his chest and was breathing very heavily. He looked strangely exhausted.

KUK-KUK-KUK-KUK . . .

Down we went into the darkness. Before long there was so little light we could hardly see our hands in front of our faces. Still the cage kept going down . . .

. . . down . . .

. . . down . . .

. . . until finally we reached the bottom. It was completely black. There was a loud scraping noise from the top of the cage, followed by a sound identical to the one that had accompanied our descent.

"He unhooked the chain," I heard Spuckler say in the darkness. "He's leavin' us down here with no way t' get back up."

Mr. Beeba moaned.

"Hang on, everybody," Spuckler said. "I'll switch on Gax's torch."

K'CHAK-FRIIING!

There was a long pause. It was still very, very dark.

"Gax," whispered Spuckler. "What's the problem?"

"THAT'S NOT MY TORCH, SIR," Gax answered apologetically. "IT'S MY TOASTER OVEN."

"Hang on."

K'CHAK-SPROING!

"How about that?" Spuckler asked.

"MY ELECTRIC SHOE POLISHER, SIR," Gax answered in the darkness.

"Hmpf!" Spuckler responded. "Remind me t' have that removed."

K'CHAK-FRAWWWWWWW!

There was a sudden flash of light as Spuckler switched on Gax's torch.

"That's more like it!" he said, grinning for what seemed like the first time in many hours. "Now at least we can see what we're up against."

The curved walls of the pit surrounded us just a yard or two beyond the iron bars of the cage. It was cold and—even with Gax's torch burning its brightest—very dark. There was a faint dripping noise somewhere nearby, but otherwise it was silent.

"I wonder what they intend to do to us down here," Mr. Beeba said, staring gloomily at the stone walls.

"I figure they aim t' keep us down here till we starve to death," Spuckler answered, sounding oddly upbeat about the idea.

"I sincerely doubt it, Spuckler," Mr. Beeba answered.

"Starvation is such a tedious form of execution. I expect these two will have come up with something a good bit more *dramatic.*"

I sat there with my knees pulled up against my chest, staring first at Spuckler, then at Mr. Beeba, then back at Spuckler again. I don't know what happened at that moment, but something inside me—something way deep down inside me—something just snapped.

"You guys aren't my friends," I heard myself say, startled by the blunt sound of the words. "You guys aren't my friends at *all.*"

"Why, Akiko—" Mr. Beeba began.

"If you *were* my friends," I interrupted, "you wouldn't have lied to me about Alia Rellapor. You would have told me the truth way back when this mission started instead of treating me like some kind of dumb little kid!"

I was vaguely aware that tears were running down my face.

" 'Kiko," Spuckler said, stretching an arm out toward me.

"Don't touch me!" I shouted, pulling back and rubbing the tears out of my eyes. Though my vision was blurry, I could see Poog staring at me with a look of great concern.

"And you're no better!" I cried hoarsely, pointing a finger at a very astonished-looking Poog. "You've known what was going on this whole time, and you told me nothing. *Nothing!*"

"Akiko, you mustn't speak to Poog this way," Mr. Beeba said urgently, sounding genuinely alarmed.

"I don't care!" I said, thrusting my face into my folded arms. I wanted so badly to be back home, miles and miles away from this awful mess. . . .

There was a very long pause. I could hear nothing but the tiny dripping sound and Gax's torch occasionally sputtering as it burned. I kept my face covered with my arms, as if by not allowing myself to see anything I might somehow magically disappear.

"You're right, 'Kiko," said Spuckler finally, his voice so quiet it was almost a whisper. "Right about one thing, anyway. We shoulda told ya 'bout Alia. Orders or no orders. We shoulda told ya."

"Yes," Mr. Beeba agreed, sighing deeply. "King Froptoppit thought that the mission would seem less . . . well, less *complicated* if you weren't told the truth about Alia.

"He was wrong about that, though," he continued after a pause, "and so were we. I can only hope that you will find it in your heart to forgive us, Akiko. For we are sorry. Terribly, terribly sorry."

There was another long pause as I sat there, taking all this in. Part of me wanted to just forgive them and forget about it. Another part of me, though, was still very angry.

"Less complicated?" I asked, sniffling.

Silence. Then:

"Yes, Akiko," said Mr. Beeba. "The truth is, King Froptoppit and Alia Rellapor were once a very happy couple. Their marriage was the envy of the galaxy. When Prince Froptoppit was born, their joy only intensified. Smoo's royal family was the picture of contentment."

I raised my head to look at Mr. Beeba. He had a distant look in his eyes as he recalled those happier times.

"Then, strangely enough, Alia began to change. No

one is quite sure why. She became bitter. Greedy. She
began to berate King Froptoppit, making many of the
claims you heard just a moment ago—that he was too
weak. That a good king must dominate his subjects
mercilessly. Needless to say, the changes in Alia began
to put a strain upon their marriage. We all hoped it was
just a passing phase, but it seemed only to get worse.

"One morning King Froptoppit awoke to find Alia
gone. She left a note saying that she had gone off to
build a castle of her own in the mountains, a dominion
from which she would one day show us all the meaning
of real power. For a time she had a large army of

devoted followers, but one by one they defected and fell away. She was simply too cruel to inspire loyalty for very long. I suppose this Throck fellow is the only one left on her side now. Throck and an army of robots."

Beeba turned to look at me, the distant look in his eyes giving way to an expression of great seriousness.

"Then, less than a year ago, a small battalion of Alia's robots descended on King Froptoppit's palace. The good people of Smoo battled tirelessly in the King's defense, but it was no use. At the end of the day the Prince was cornered in the palace gardens, captured, and taken off to Alia's castle. King Froptoppit sent rescue party after rescue party, but to no avail. That's when he turned to you, Akiko."

I stared at Spuckler and Mr. Beeba, then at Gax and Poog. They were all looking at me anxiously, waiting to see how I'd react.

I suppose I should have been shocked or angry or something. Oddly enough, I was just relieved. Relieved to have finally heard the truth. A lot of it still didn't make any sense to me, but at least I felt pretty sure I wasn't being lied to anymore.

"Apology accepted," I said.

Mr. Beeba and Spuckler both sighed their relief. Poog also looked very pleased, though not at all surprised.

"But let me make one thing clear," I said, looking very sternly at Spuckler and Mr. Beeba. "I don't ever want to catch you keeping secrets from me again. Do you understand me? *Never.*"

"I hear ya, 'Kiko," Spuckler said. "Loud an' clear."

"Absolutely," Mr. Beeba chimed in. "Spuckler and I have learned our lesson. Truly we have."

"Just one thing, Mr. Beeba."

"Yes, Akiko?"

"Lend me your handkerchief, will you?" I said. "My nose is running like crazy."

Chapter 15

After a moment there was a strange rumbling sound. I felt the cage rattling beneath me as if we were in the midst of a minor earthquake.

"MY MOTION DETECTORS, SIR——" Gax began.

"Yeah, I know, Gax," Spuckler interrupted. "I feel it too."

"What's going on?" I asked, staring nervously into the darkness.

"This is it!" Mr. Beeba announced in a panicked voice. "Execution time!"

"Beebs!" Spuckler cried. "Get ahold of yourself!"

Just then I noticed that the temperature seemed to be

rising. I thought it might have just been Gax's torch, but eventually I could tell that it was coming from somewhere outside the cage.

"A lava trap," Spuckler muttered. "I mighta known."

"*A lava trap?*" Mr. Beeba repeated, his voice loud and shrill.

"Wh-what's a lava trap?" I asked, hoping it wasn't as self-explanatory as it sounded.

"Well, basically," Spuckler explained, "it's a trap where they get ya in some place where ya can't get back out—like this here pit, for instance—an' then what they do is dump a buncha lava on ya. Hurts pretty bad, I 'magine."

"*Hurts pretty bad?*" Mr. Beeba repeated, sounding even more panicked than before. "You mean *kills* pretty bad!"

"Well," Spuckler answered, rubbing his chin thoughtfully, "yeah, Beebs, if ya wanna get technical."

I stared up in horror as I saw tiny streaks of glowing yellow-and-orange lava begin to trickle down the walls from somewhere high above. In seconds big puddles of the stuff began forming where the walls met the floor, slowly creeping in toward the cage, inch by inch.

"We're going to be buried alive!" Mr. Beeba shrieked. "We're going to be *burned* alive!" He paused, then added, "We're going to be buried alive *and* burned alive!"

"Oh no we ain't," Spuckler announced confidently.

He reached inside Gax and produced a tool about the size of an eggbeater. At one end of the tool was a small rotary blade. Clicking a button on one side, Spuckler made the blade spin at an incredible speed.

"Cover your eyes, now," Spuckler said to Mr. Beeba and me. "This thing tends to send out a lotta sparks."

I turned my face away and covered my eyes with my hands.

ZZZZYYYYAAAAAAAAAAARRRRRRRRRR!!!

There was a terrible grinding sound. I wanted to see what Spuckler was doing, but I didn't dare look. There were two loud clanking noises, like the sound of a barbell being dropped on a metal floor. Ten or twenty seconds later the noise stopped and Spuckler invited us to see what he had done.

Two bars of the cage had been cut away, creating a window about three feet tall and two feet wide.

"C'mon, everybody!" Spuckler shouted. "Up on top of the cage! Fast as ya can!"

By then the pools of lava on the floor had reached the bottom of the cage and begun to seep between the bars. I stuck my foot into Spuckler's folded hands and stepped up through the opening he had made.

When I got to the top of the cage, I saw that the chain was gone, just as Spuckler had said. Peering up into the darkness, I could see a tiny circle of light in the distance. It looked as if we were at least half a mile away from the top of the pit.

"Akiko! Do give me a hand here, won't you?"

It was Mr. Beeba. His head was poking out from under the roof of the cage, a look of real terror gripping his face. I reached down with both hands and helped him up. Spuckler lifted Gax by his round robot body and carefully handed him to us before swiftly scrambling up himself. By then the floor of the cage was completely covered with white-hot lava, which created an intense dry heat beneath us. It was like being trapped inside a parked car with all the windows up on a blistering August day. We quickly peeled off our thick winter coats and allowed them to fall into the glowing fire beneath us.

"We're doomed! *Doomed!*" Mr. Beeba wailed.

For once his fears seemed to be completely justified. The fiery rivers continued pouring down the walls, raising the level of the lava to ever greater heights. Within minutes the cage was more than half buried. Stranded on the top, there was nothing we could do but huddle closer and closer together.

"I just want you all to know," Mr. Beeba said tearfully, "that I can think of no people I'd rather die with than you. . . ."

"For cryin' out loud, Beebs, we ain't gonna die!" Spuckler said between clenched teeth. But even *he* seemed to have run out of ideas. We all stared longingly at the tiny circle of light hundreds of feet above, hoping that by some miracle the lava flow would stop.

It didn't.

Soon only about a foot and a half of the cage remained above the scalding-hot lava, and another inch vanished with each passing second. Wondering if this really *was* the end, I looked at Spuckler, Mr. Beeba, Gax, and . . .

I suddenly realized that Poog was nowhere to be seen.

Just then the cage began to tremble under us. At first I thought it was just being lifted by the sheer volume of the fiery material surrounding it. But no! It was actually *rising into the air,* floating up out of the lava as if by magic. Spuckler lay down and stuck his head out over the edge of the cage.

"It's Poog!" he shouted. "He's underneath this here cage!"

He swung his head around and gave us a big toothy grin just as the cage broke free of the lava for good.

"He's liftin' us outta here!" Spuckler hollered, cackling with delight.

Mr. Beeba and I held on for dear life as Poog carried the cage—and all of us on top of it—from the very bottom of the pit to the very top. The bricks on the wall raced by as we kept going up, up, up. I sucked in the clean, cool air with hungry gulps as the cage rose over the lip of the hole and settled gently on one side of the room.

Throck was gone. So were the Torgs.

We scrambled down from the top of the cage to see if Poog was all right. He looked very tired but happy. I reached out and gave him a big hug. (Don't ask me how you hug an alien that has no arms. You just *do* it.)

"Thank you, Poog! Thank you!"

Mr. Beeba, Spuckler, and Gax all joined in congratulating Poog. I'd always suspected that Poog was the most important member of our team. Now I knew for sure.

chapter 16

We were all so happy and relieved just to be alive, I don't think it had occurred to us that we'd need a plan once we'd made it out of the hole.

" 'Kiko, I reckon it's up to you," Spuckler said when our little celebration was over. "Should we try t' rescue the Prince again, or should we jus' hightail it on outta here?"

"Yes, Akiko," said Mr. Beeba. "In view of the, er, *revelations* regarding Alia Rellapor, perhaps you've had to reassess your attitude toward the mission?"

He was right. Knowing that Alia Rellapor was the Prince's mother changed everything. After all, she had as much right to keep the Prince with her as the King did. But she was locking him up in that horrible little room all day! What was she, crazy? Then again, the Prince had said he was getting all the food he needed. Maybe she was just trying to toughen him up, as she'd said. It was a very difficult decision.

"Well, guys," I said at last, "I hate to say it, but I think we've just got to give up the mission and get out of here. I don't like Alia Rellapor any more than you do. But she *is* the Prince's mother, and as long as she's not *hurting* him, I guess she can raise him any way she likes."

Spuckler looked disappointed, but he nodded his agreement. Mr. Beeba looked very relieved.

"It's agreed, then," Mr. Beeba announced. "Our mission is at an end. Now we must focus all our energies on getting out of this infernal castle."

So we all crept back down the hallway toward Alia Rellapor's chambers. I kept half expecting Throck to jump out and grab us, but he seemed to have disappeared, at least for the time being. When we neared Alia's throne room, Gax went ahead and took a peek to make sure the coast was clear.

"THE THRONE IS EMPTY, AS IS THE ROOM," Gax told us in a mechanical whisper. "NO ALIA. NO THROCK. NO TORGS."

"Well, c'mon then," Spuckler said impatiently. "Let's go."

We tiptoed along the edge of the wall toward the heavy red curtain at the back of the room. Before we got there, though, Poog noticed something. He spoke quickly, in his warbly garbled language, stopping us in our tracks.

"What is it?" I asked. "Throck?"

"No," Mr. Beeba. "It's Alia. She's somewhere in this room. Poog says . . . But no, I must have misheard him."

Poog spoke again, saying what sounded like the same thing, only he said it a bit more loudly and insistently.

"Come on, Beebs!" Spuckler whispered. "What's he sayin'?"

"He says . . . ," Mr. Beeba began, his eyes squinting in disbelief, "Poog says *Alia needs our help*."

"What?" Spuckler and I asked simultaneously.

"I know, I know!" Mr. Beeba said, pointing defensively at Poog. "It doesn't make any sense to me, either! But that's what Poog said, and he seems quite convinced of the idea."

"Well, let's find her and see what Poog's talking about," I said. The idea of Alia Rellapor's needing our help seemed beyond ridiculous, but I'd learned by now never to doubt Poog.

Upon searching the room, we found a small, dark alcove off to one side. There, on a large rectangular block of marble, lay Alia Rellapor, sound asleep. She was on her back with her hands folded across her chest, like Sleeping Beauty in the old fairy tale. Her face was almost drained of color, though, so she also looked a bit like a vampire.

A very *pretty* vampire.

"What's going on?" I whispered. "What's wrong with her?"

Poog floated over to my side. He looked very strange all of a sudden. He turned to face me and gazed deeply into my eyes.

Bit by bit the room seemed to tilt, first to one side, then to the other. My body began to feel very sleepy, but my mind had never been so wide awake. I was vaguely aware of Mr. Beeba and Gax and Spuckler, but they seemed to fall away into the distance while Poog expanded to fill my entire field of vision.

What happened next is almost impossible to describe.

It was as if Poog were sending images directly into my brain. I could see them in front of my eyes, but I could also see them inside my head. It was like dreaming and being awake at the same time.

I could see Alia Rellapor. She looked younger, happier. She was back at the palace with King Froptoppit and the Prince, smiling, laughing, perfectly content. Then I saw Throck. He was also younger, with less armor and machinery covering his body. I saw him staring at Alia Rellapor from somewhere outside the palace. I saw him mixing potions and casting spells like some kind of warlock or voodoo doctor: chanting, whispering, sometimes shouting.

Suddenly it became very clear to me: Alia wasn't evil. She had been *made* evil. She was being controlled by *Throck!*

I wanted to tell everyone my discovery, but Poog wasn't finished with me yet. He kept sending images into my brain. Now I saw scenes of our journey, little flashes of things that had happened to us before we got to Alia Rellapor's castle. I saw Spuckler throwing the stone at the Torg. I saw all of us crossing the Moonguzzit Sea on the superlong bridge. I saw myself climbing up the Great Wall of Trudd. I saw Queen Pwip. I saw Admiral Frutz. . . .

Then I saw one scene that was especially clear and vivid. Poog and I were in the forest in the middle of the night. Poog was teaching me words in his own language. It seemed so real I could almost hear the insect sounds coming from the forest and smell the wood crackling on the fire.

The words. Poog was repeating the words to me, making me memorize them. Over and over he drilled the words into my brain. I felt them forming on my tongue. I opened my mouth. I heard the words coming out, echoing off the walls.

The *walls*?

I opened my eyes. I was back in Alia Rellapor's castle. Spuckler and Mr. Beeba were looking at me with great astonishment.

"Heavens!" Mr. Beeba said. "Well, I'll be dagnabbed!" Spuckler said, rubbing the back of his neck agitatedly with one hand.

Poog was gazing at me with supreme pride.

"What?" I asked. *"What?"*

"Akiko, my dear child," Mr. Beeba said. "You just said something in Poog's language. You said it loudly. And with a *very* convincing accent, I must say."

I shook myself vigorously. It was as if I'd just come back from a very long journey.

Chapter 17

"Where am I?"

It took us a moment to realize that Alia Rellapor had asked the question. She was awake but still lying flat on her back on the big block of marble. There was something different about her voice. It was softer and a little weak, but also more natural and relaxed-sounding.

We all remained silent. I don't think any of us knew quite what to say to her.

"Mr. Beeba!" Alia said, straining to turn her head toward him. "Is that *you*?"

"Yes, that's right," Mr. Beeba said with a confused

look on his face. "Are you quite all right, Alia? You look gravely ill."

"I feel . . . I feel *weak*," she answered.

"Don't worry, Alia," I said to her. "You've just woken up from some sort of trance."

Spuckler and Mr. Beeba stared at me with blank expressions, clearly not understanding a word I'd said.

"Wh-who *are* you?" Alia asked, rising on her elbows to get a better look at me. "Where did you come from?"

"My name is Akiko," I answered, seeing from the look on her face that she had no memory of our earlier meeting. "I come from . . . well, it's a long story. I'm sure we'll have time to talk about that later. Right now we've got to get you out of here, you and your son."

"My son?" Alia asked, a look of alarm coming over her face. "Where is he?"

Mr. Beeba and Spuckler were thoroughly confused. How could Alia not know where her son was? Me, I knew better. I figured Alia probably had no memory of *anything* that had happened in a very long time.

There was a sudden burst of garbled syllables as Poog said something to all of us. I couldn't understand what it was, but somehow it seemed a little more—I don't know—*familiar* than it had been before.

"Heavens!" cried Mr. Beeba. "It's Throck! He's preparing to leave Smoo at this very moment. An escape ship is docked and waiting for him at the other end of the castle. And that's not all," he added. *"He's taking the Prince with him!"*

"No!" I cried. "We've got to stop him!"

Poog opened his mouth and produced another string of garbled sounds, this time staring intently at me.

"Quickly, Akiko!" Mr. Beeba shouted. "Get on top of Poog!"

"On *top* of him?" I asked.

"This is no time for questions, Akiko! Do as he says!"

Mr. Beeba was pushing me from behind with both hands, forcing me over to a spot where Poog was floating just a few feet above the floor. I put both my hands on top of Poog's head and hoisted myself up, resting my stomach squarely on top of him.

"Hang on tight, 'Kiko!" Spuckler called out as Poog lifted me ten or fifteen feet into the air. "The Poog Express is fixin' t' fly!"

With that, Poog carried me straight across the room. I struggled to keep my balance as we blew through the heavy red curtain and across the throne room. Zipping through the nearest doorway, Poog carried me through a maze of corridors at lightning speed. I wished he would slow down a little, but he only flew faster and faster. Hallways and staircases sailed past in a blur. (To tell the truth, if I hadn't been scared half to death, I'd probably have thought it was a lot of fun!)

After a few more minutes of zooming this way and that, we suddenly came to a stop near an open-air platform in one of the highest parts of the castle. Snow-capped peaks stood in the distance beneath a cloudless

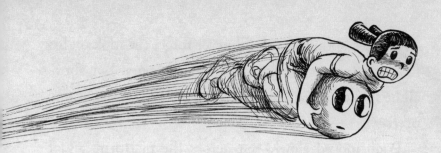

sky of pale blue. The tops of several towers were visible below. We must have been sixty or seventy stories up. I climbed off Poog and stood there at the base of the platform. An icy breeze blew across my arms, and I immediately regretted having thrown my coat into the lava.

The platform was about ten feet wide and built of white stone. It jutted out into the air a hundred feet or so, like a bridge leading to nowhere. At the very end of the platform was a spaceship. It was about the size of a small school bus, floating in midair like a boat moored to a dock. Throck was about halfway across the platform. He had Prince Froptoppit tucked under one arm and was walking briskly toward the spaceship. The Prince lifted his head and saw me.

"Akiko!" he shouted.

Throck spun around. I'll never forget the look on his face. He looked shocked. He looked angry. But above all he looked *scared*. Not scared of me, of course. Scared of *Poog*.

Poog moved slowly out across the platform, and I cautiously followed him. The wind blew so hard my arms felt numb. Remembering what had happened to me on the Great Wall of Trudd, I ordered myself not to look down. And believe it or not, I actually managed to follow my own order. But I couldn't help being aware of how high up in the air we were. There were no guardrails or anything! Fearing that one good gust of wind would be the end of me, I bent my knees as much as I could and kept very low to the surface of the platform.

Throck just stood there, waiting, the Prince firmly gripped under one arm. Every so often his heavily armored suit sent up a huge cloud of steam that was immediately carried off by the wind.

HHSSSSSSHHHH!

When we reached a spot ten or fifteen feet away from Throck, I came to a stop, allowing Poog to float forward until he was just a few feet from Throck's face. As they faced each other, I sensed that years and years of conflict had brought them to this place. One thing was for sure: This time, Poog was *not* going to negotiate.

From where I stood I had a pretty good view of Throck's face. He looked tired and frightened, as if he were about to give up. I think he knew he was no match for Poog. For a minute there I thought he was going to just hand the Prince over and beg for mercy. But then his eyes widened and a sort of panic seized his face. Twisting his body back to one side, he gripped the Prince fiercely with both hands. Then he threw him off the platform.

Chapter 18

"Nooooo!" I cried, watching helplessly as Prince Froptoppit flipped through the air.

Poog didn't waste a second. He shot down after the Prince, racing against gravity to catch him before he hit the ground. I was watching breathlessly to see if he'd get there in time when suddenly I felt icy fingers close around my neck.

HHSSSSSSSSSHHHHH!

"Say goodbye to your beloved Prince, little girl," I heard Throck whisper in my ear as he lifted me into his arms, "and while you're at it, bid this wretched planet farewell. You're coming with me!"

I wanted to scream, but my throat was suddenly so dry I could barely make a sound.

"Relax, my child," he said as he carried me over to the spaceship, opened the hatch, and tossed me roughly inside. "Soon we will be far, far away from here."

Time seemed to slow down as I watched Throck step into the ship after me and reach up to close the hatch. I stared back across the platform toward the castle. Poog and the Prince were nowhere to be seen. The hatch was halfway closed. Three-quarters closed . . .

I don't know what made me do it. Maybe it was Poog communicating with me or something. Maybe it was just total desperation.

I opened my mouth and said the words Poog had taught me back in the forest, the words that had brought Alia Rellapor out of her trance. They came out as little more than a hoarse whisper, but the effect on Throck was immediate and devastating. He shuddered, groaned, and let go of the hatch. Then he dropped to his knees and crawled back onto the platform.

There, just over Throck's shoulder, I saw the Prince rise slowly over the edge of the platform, holding on to

Poog with both hands. If Throck had his eyes open at that moment, it was probably the last thing he saw.

We all stared in horror as Throck came grinding to a halt. Bit by bit the color of his skin faded to gray. Then the color of his armor also drained away, and within seconds Throck was entirely covered in ghostly gray from head to toe.

He had turned to stone.

The Prince ran over and gave me the biggest hug his little arms were capable of.

"Thank you, Akiko!" he cried, his voice trembling with emotion. "Thank you!"

We both walked cautiously over to Throck and joined Poog in examining him up close. When I touched his body, it felt as cold and hard as a statue. As far as I could tell, it *was* a statue.

"Did . . . did I *kill* him?" I asked.

Poog smiled and said something in his warbly language. I couldn't understand exactly what he said, but somehow I knew that the answer was no. Perhaps I'd just frozen Throck into this form temporarily. Poog said something else, then turned and flew back into the castle.

"He must be going to get the others," I said to Prince Froptoppit.

He had a slightly sad look on his face, as if he'd just recalled something that was troubling him.

"Akiko," he said to me, "did you see my mother? Is she going to be okay?"

"I'm pretty sure she will be, Prince Froptoppit," I said. "She's been through a lot, just like you have. But everything's going to be okay now. I can feel that in my heart."

And I *could*, too. All the tension and fear and misery of the past few hours had suddenly melted away. For the first time in a very long time, I felt as if I could just relax.

The Prince and I ran back to the base of the platform. The wind was a little less strong there, but it was still pretty cold. Prince Froptoppit took off his white cape and gave it to me to wrap around myself. He was very shy about it, but also very gentlemanly. I pulled the cape tightly around my arms, thanking the Prince.

After a few minutes Poog returned with Spuckler, Mr. Beeba, Gax, and Alia Rellapor. When Alia saw the Prince, she hugged him as though she hadn't seen him in years.

It was then that it really hit me: We'd done it. We'd rescued the Prince. Not only that—we'd rescued his mother at the same time!

There was a brief discussion about what should be done with Throck.

"I say we should just push him off th' platform," Spuckler said, staring angrily at the strange white statue that Throck had become, "and watch him smash into a million kajillion pieces."

"I appreciate your sentiments, Spuckler," Mr. Beeba replied, "but we must keep in mind that Throck is still very much alive, immobilized though he may be in his current state."

"Maybe we should just leave him where he is, then," I said.

"No, Akiko," Mr. Beeba replied. "The spell you've cast upon him won't last indefinitely. I believe we should take him back with us to the palace. He must be carefully preserved and allowed to atone for his transgressions. With any luck, he may eventually learn his lesson and renounce his evil ways."

"So how are we going to *get* back to the palace?" I asked. "Don't tell me we have to go back and climb the Great Wall of Trudd again!"

"Oh dear, Akiko," Mr. Beeba replied, scratching his head and pacing back and forth. "I hadn't thought of that."

"With all due respect," said Alia Rellapor, "I believe the answer is right before our eyes." She pointed a finger in the direction of Throck's escape ship, still hovering at the end of the platform.

"I was kinda hopin' you'd say that, Alia," Spuckler said with a sly grin as he trotted across the platform to take a better look at the ship. "I've always wanted to get behind the wheel of one of these!"

The only thing left to do was to carry Throck from the end of the platform into the hull of the ship. Together Spuckler, Mr. Beeba, the Prince, and I had just enough muscle to get Throck's stony mass on board.

Once we were all inside the ship with the hatch closed, everyone seemed to relax into a celebratory mood. Spuckler got the ship moving, and soon he and Mr. Beeba were bickering about one thing or another, just as they always did, only this time they really seemed to be *enjoying* themselves. Alia and the Prince chattered happily about all the good food they'd have once they got back to the palace. Poog sang a little tune for us, a cheerful melody that seemed to chase away any fears or worries that might have remained. I sat back in a heavily padded chair in the back of the ship, closed my eyes, and almost immediately nodded off to sleep.

It had been a *very* long day.

Chapter 19

The flight back to the palace took many hours—all night long, in fact—but it was mercifully uneventful. I woke to the sound of Mr. Beeba and Poog talking to one another in excited but hushed tones. They were evidently at the end of a very long and intense discussion.

"So *that's* why Alia acted so strangely," said Mr. Beeba, rubbing his forehead thoughtfully. "I can't believe I never saw it before. It all seems so *obvious* now."

Spuckler called back to us from the cockpit, announcing that we were a mere half hour away from the palace.

"I'll believe it when I see it," Mr. Beeba sneered, sounding as if even *then* he wouldn't believe it. And who could blame him? We'd experienced so many setbacks during the past week that it hardly seemed possible our journey could end so smoothly.

But sure enough, about half an hour later King Froptoppit's majestic palace came into view, glowing purplish pink in the early-morning sunlight. I couldn't help thinking back to the night I'd first come here with Bip and Bop, how nervous I was, and how ignorant of what was to come. It seemed so long ago, almost as though I'd been a different person then.

Spuckler steered the ship right up to King Froptoppit's quarters and parked it at a grand marble entrance nearby. Within seconds the area was swarming with excited guards and members of the King's inner circle. A moment later King Froptoppit himself arrived, strutting forward so that he could be the very first to greet us.

As soon as the hatch was opened, Prince Froptoppit ran out and leaped into his father's arms. I'd imagined this moment for a long time. It was hard to believe it was finally coming true.

"There's my boy!" King Froptoppit said, a single tear running down his cheek, his arms firmly locked around the Prince. "I *knew* Akiko would bring you back to me! There was never a doubt in my—"

He stopped in midsentence, his eyes having fallen upon Alia Rellapor. She had just stepped out of the ship and was standing nervously between Spuckler and me. She looked very ill at ease, as if she wanted to hide under the nearest rock.

The King jumped to his feet, drawing the Prince protectively behind him.

"Arrest her, men!" he shouted, pointing a quivering finger at Alia. "This heinous crime will not go unpunished!"

A half dozen or so of King Froptoppit's guards stepped forward. Spuckler and Gax moved quickly in front of Alia, stopping the guards in their tracks. Poog also floated over until he was positioned just a few inches from Alia's shoulder. It looked as if there was going to be a standoff.

"Your Majesty, Your Majesty," Mr. Beeba said, dashing over to King Froptoppit's side, using a very practiced diplomatic tone. "I'm afraid there are a great many things you don't know about Alia. I would strongly recommend a bit of *debriefing* before you take any action against her."

King Froptoppit's look of anger dissolved into an expression of mild confusion.

"Yes, yes, I see," he whispered to Mr. Beeba, never taking his eyes off Alia. "Let's hear it, then."

Mr. Beeba stepped into an area between all the parties concerned and began a very calm and measured explanation of events as he understood them. He was

like a lawyer making his case before a jury, raising first one hand and then the other, underlining the importance of certain words with the stroke of a finger, squinting his eyes nearly closed at times and throwing them open wide at others. I didn't think I'd ever seen him so . . . well, so much *in his element* before. He was clearly enjoying himself.

He told King Froptoppit how Alia had been bewitched by Throck, who was the last surviving member of an evil society called the Mulgari. Obsessed with power and preaching a doctrine of rule by force, they were the worst sort of cowards and were absolutely terrified of the responsibilities of leadership. They used their spells and trances to manipulate others into doing their dirty work for them, while they stood safely in the shadows.

Mr. Beeba finished his presentation by leading King Froptoppit into the hull of the ship and showing him Throck's frozen stone body, explaining how Poog and I had managed to save the Prince in the end. The King thanked both of us graciously and then turned at last to the woman he had long believed was his foe.

"Alia," King Froptoppit said, walking slowly and somewhat sheepishly over to her. "It seems I owe you an apology. . . ."

Without a word Alia stepped forward and threw her arms around King Froptoppit's neck. All at once they seemed a very happy couple, just as they must have been long ago.

"And here I was thinking you'd turned against me because of that little spat we'd had," I heard King Froptoppit say.

"What spat?" I asked.

"Oh, it was just a silly little misunderstanding, Akiko," Alia explained with a smile. "I'm sure we can hardly even remember what it was about now, can we, dear?"

"Indeed," the King agreed, chuckling. "A laughably trivial matter, as I recall."

"Now hang on a minute, here," I said, planting my hands firmly on my hips. "We've gone through an awful lot of trouble to get the two of you back together. I want some details on this little spat of yours."

"Yes, well . . . ," King Froptoppit began, turning to Alia with a look of mild discomfort, ". . . correct me if I'm wrong, dear, but it was something about my last name not being quite *good* enough for you, wasn't it?"

"Come now," Alia answered very matter-of-factly, turning to address everyone present, "I'm sure you'd all agree that 'Alia Froptoppit' doesn't have nearly the same *lilt* as 'Alia Rellapor.' "

"I think 'Froptoppit' has an *abundance* of lilt," the King answered with an angry snort.

"Okay, okay, I get the general idea!" I said. "Look, you two have got to *watch* it with these little spats. That's when guys like Throck step in and turn everything upside down!"

King Froptoppit walked toward me, dropped down on one knee, and placed his hands on my shoulders.

"You're quite right, Akiko," he said very solemnly. "*Quite* right. Alia and I owe you a debt of gratitude that can never be fully repaid. Indeed, you've done more than just reunite our family. You've saved the planet Smoo from tyranny!"

He stopped and took several big sniffs with his oversized nose.

SHNIFF SHNIFF SHNIFF.

"Ahem," he coughed, rising to his feet. "Now don't take this personally, but I'm ordering all of you to the royal bathhouses to be, er, *freshened up* a bit."

Mr. Beeba, Spuckler, and I all stared at each other and blushed. Let's face it: Five days without a bath doesn't do much for a person's body odor. We were all *seriously* stinky.

"When you're done with that, we will reconvene in the royal gardens," King Froptoppit announced, his voice now filled with gleeful anticipation. "Today there will be a celebration in this palace the likes of which you've never seen!"

Chapter 20

The rest of the day was a bit of a blur. I was escorted to the royal bathhouses by a team of heavyset women who led me from one scented, steamy pool to the next. One of them washed my hair, another scrubbed my feet, and yet another filed my nails. Finally they just let me soak for a while in a hot tub that swirled gently around me like a slow-motion whirlpool.

While I was in the baths, someone had washed and pressed my T-shirt and jeans and all my other clothes (they even replaced my shoelaces!), so when I got dressed I felt as clean and fresh as the night I'd left home. Even cleaner, really, if you want to know the truth.

I was then led out to the royal gardens, which were every bit as gorgeous as Prince Froptoppit had said. There were trees of every size and shape and flowers of every color. In the middle of the garden was an enormous yellow tent stretched over table after table of delicious-looking food. A large band of musicians was making beautiful but very unusual music, like a symphony slowly being played backward.

In the center of everything stood a big round table for the guests of honor. Spuckler was there, having

evidently just received a shave and a haircut. He looked very handsome but very embarrassed to be so clean! Mr. Beeba was dressed in some sort of official robe, with matching gloves and a very scholarly-looking hat. Gax had been polished up as clean as they could make him. (Actually I couldn't see much of a difference, but at least they'd tried.) And of course Poog was there too. I don't know if he'd been given a bath or not, but he certainly looked happy and very proud.

The gates of the gardens were thrown open so that

all the people of Smoo could join in the festivities. The band played tune after tune, songs that flowed seamlessly from one melody to the next. Couples danced and children played games. Royal stewards brought tray after tray of hot food and sparkling juices in dozens of colors. I ate and ate until I couldn't eat another bite.

King Froptoppit, Alia Rellapor, and the Prince came by our table to thank us again and again. The King invited me to stay a few more days on Smoo, but I told him I thought it was really time for me to go back home.

Home! I'd been so busy with everything I'd almost stopped *thinking* of home. Would I really be able to go there soon?

As the evening sun went down, the party continued, but I asked King Froptoppit if I could leave early.

"I've had so much fun today, King Froptoppit," I told him, "but I need to sleep in my own bed tonight, if you know what I mean."

"I understand, Akiko," he answered with a sad-looking smile. "But you must promise to come back soon. We're all going to miss you terribly, you know."

All my friends from Smoo walked along with me as I headed toward the ship that would take me home. It was a little round blue-and-red-and-yellow ship, just like the one that had brought me here.

"Don't forget to write," Mr. Beeba said, not bothering to explain how I was supposed to send a letter all the way from another galaxy.

"An' don't work too hard at school," Spuckler advised, drawing an angry glance from Mr. Beeba.

"YOU *WILL* COME BACK TO SEE US AGAIN, MA'AM, WON'T YOU?" Gax asked, his squeaky mechanical voice sounding unusually emotional.

"Definitely, Gax" I answered. "This isn't the last you'll see of me, I promise."

Alia Rellapor and the Prince thanked me one last time for everything I'd done. So did Spuckler and Mr. Beeba and everyone else. By the end of it I was just about ready to cry. My throat felt all choked up and my hands were shaking. I gave everyone a hug, one at a time, and finally made my way to the back of the ship.

I climbed aboard and waved goodbye to everyone as Bip and Bop revved up the engines. The little ship rose from the platform, and soon I was presented with a dazzling view of the palace just as the sun sank behind the horizon. Everyone waved to me from below, and I kept my eyes on them for as long as I could before they disappeared from sight.

I sank into the backseat as we continued rising into the air, and I sighed deeply. Only then did I realize Poog was there beside me.

He smiled at me, saying goodbye in his own quiet way. I leaned over and gave him one last hug. I must

have held him next to me for more than a minute. Then I let go and watched him float back from me a foot or two. He blinked once or twice, smiled again, and then zipped away into the cool evening air. I watched him go back toward the palace in a long slow arc. Soon the entire planet was visible from our little ship; then it grew smaller and smaller and finally became indistinguishable from the all the stars around it.

I was on my way home.

Chapter 21

There's not a whole lot to say about what it was like to get home. I was expecting this really big—I don't know—*feeling* when I got back to my bedroom. It wasn't like that, though. It was just as if I'd never left. Everything was exactly the same.

The Akiko robot came over and opened the window and we traded places without anyone seeing us. Before she left, I asked her if people had become suspicious of her or if anyone had figured out that she wasn't the real Akiko. She said she didn't think so, but that Melissa was surprised at how good I'd become at building card houses all of a sudden. And my parents had commented on how I'd started eating more vegetables than I used to.

"Oh, great," I replied. "Did you tell my parents you were going to stop watching TV while you were at it?"

"No," she answered with a smile. "I thought I'd leave that up to you."

A moment later she was gone, and Bip and Bop with her. All at once it was very, very quiet.

I took a peek out into the hallway. I could hear my father snoring. Or maybe it was my mother. (They *both* snore, can you believe it?) I went back to my room and spent a few minutes just looking at all my stuff: my schoolbooks, my Japanese dolls, the half-finished jigsaw puzzle I'd stopped working on months before.

It was good to be back home. But it was also kind of weird. It was as if I'd gotten *used* to being on Smoo. I half expected to turn around and find Spuckler and Mr. Beeba in my closet, arguing about what I ought to wear to school the next day.

It was hard to get to sleep that night. I kept wonder-

ing about things on Smoo, and what was going on there, and whether they'd be coming back to get me sometime in the future.

After a few days, though, things slowly went back to normal. Soon I could go hours without thinking about Smoo, even whole days. Sure, sometimes I'd be sitting in the middle of Mr. Moylan's class at Middleton Elementary and suddenly get this uncontrollable urge to stand up and shout, "Hey, everybody! I've been to another planet!" But, thinking it through, I knew there was simply no point in making everyone think I was crazy.

In the end I guess I've gone back to being an ordinary kid again. But hey, there's nothing wrong with being an ordinary kid, is there? I mean, I *like* it here on Earth, I really do. Take it from me: Nothing makes you appreciate this planet like being taken somewhere *else* for a few days.

But I'd be lying if I said I wouldn't like to get another letter someday, inviting me back to the planet Smoo. I would. And if I do, well, let me tell you: I'll be right there at my window at eight o'clock, ready to go.

See where it all began in

on the Planet Smoo

Join Akiko and her crew on the Planet Smoo!

When fourth grader Akiko comes home from school one day, she finds an envelope waiting for her. It has no stamp or return address and contains a *very* strange message. . . .

At first Akiko thinks the message is a joke, but before she knows it, she's heading a rescue mission to find the King of Smoo's kidnapped son, Prince Frop-toppit. Akiko, the head of a rescue mission? She's too afraid to be on the school's safety patrol!

Read the following excerpt from *Akiko on the Planet Smoo* and see how the adventure began.

Excerpt from *Akiko on the Planet Smoo* copyright © 2000 by Mark Crilley
Akiko on the Planet Smoo
Published by Delacorte Press
an imprint of Random House Children's Books
a division of Random House, Inc.
1540 Broadway, New York, New York 10036
Reprinted by arrangement with Delacorte Press

Chapter 1

My name is Akiko. This is the story of the adventure I had a few months ago when I went to the planet Smoo. I know it's kind of hard to believe, but it really did happen. I swear.

I'd better go back to the beginning: the day I got the letter.

It was a warm, sunny day. There were only about five weeks left before summer vacation, and kids at school were already itching to get out. Everybody was talking about how they'd be going to camp, or some really cool amusement park, or whatever. Me, I knew I'd be staying right here in Middleton all summer, which was just fine by me. My dad works at a company where they hardly ever get long vacations, so my mom and I have kind of gotten used to it.

Anyway, it was after school and my best friend, Melissa, and I had just walked home together as always. Most of the other kids get picked up by their parents or take the bus, but Melissa and I live close enough to walk to school every day. We both live just a few blocks away in this big apartment building that must have been built about a hundred years ago. Actually I think it used to be an office building or something, but then somebody cleaned it up and turned it into this fancy new apartment building. It's all red bricks and tall windows, with a big black fire escape in the back. My parents say they'd rather live somewhere out in the suburbs, but my dad has to be near his office downtown.

Melissa lives on the sixth floor but she usually comes up with me to the seventeenth floor after school. She's got three younger brothers and has to share her bedroom with one of them, so she doesn't get a whole lot of privacy. I'm an only child and I've got a pretty big bedroom all to myself, so that's where Melissa and I spend a lot of our time.

On that day we were in my room as usual, listening to the radio and trying our best to make some decent card houses. Melissa was telling me how cool it would be if I became the new captain of the fourth-grade safety patrol.

"Come on, Akiko, it'll be good for you," she said. "I practically promised Mrs. Miller that you'd do it."

"Melissa, why can't somebody *else* be in charge of the safety patrol?" I replied. "I'm no good at that kind of stuff. Remember what happened when Mrs. Antwerp gave me the lead role in the Christmas show?"

Melissa usually knows how to make me feel better about things, but even she had to admit last year's Christmas show was a big disaster.

"That was different, Akiko," she insisted. "Mrs. Antwerp had no idea you were going to get stage fright like that."

"It was worse than stage fright, Melissa," I said. "I can't believe I actually forgot the words to 'Jingle Bells.'"

"This isn't the Christmas show," she said. "You don't

have to memorize any words to be in charge of the safety patrol." She was carefully beginning the third floor of a very ambitious card house she'd been working on for about half an hour.

"Why can't I just be a *member* of the safety patrol?" I asked her.

"Because Mrs. Miller needs a leader," she said. "I'd do it, but I'm already in charge of the softball team."

And I knew Melissa meant it, too. She'd be in charge of *everything* at school if she could. Me, I prefer to let someone else be the boss. Sure, there are times when I wish I could be the one who makes all the decisions and tells everybody else what to do. I just don't want to be the one who gets in trouble when everything goes wrong.

"Besides," Melissa continued, "it would be a great way for you to meet Brendan Fitzpatrick. He's in charge of the boys' safety patrol." One thing about Melissa: No matter what kind of conversation you have with her, one way or another you end up talking about boys.

"What makes you so sure I *want* to meet Brendan Fitzpatrick?" The card house I'd been working on had completely collapsed, and I was trying to decide whether it was worth the trouble to start a new one.

"Trust me, Akiko," she said with a big grin, *"everyone* wants to meet Brendan Fitzpatrick."

"I don't even like him," I said, becoming even more anxious to change the subject.

"How can you not like him?" she asked, genuinely puzzled. "He's one of the top five cute guys in the fourth grade."

"I can't believe you actually have a *list* of who's cute and who isn't."

That was when my mom knocked on my door. (I always keep the door shut when Melissa's over. I never know when she's going to say something I don't want my mom to hear.)

"Akiko, you got something in the mail," she said, handing me a small silvery envelope.

She stared at me with this very curious look in her eyes. I don't get letters very often. "Are you sure you don't want this door open?" she asked. "It's kind of stuffy in here."

"Thanks, Mom. Better keep it closed."

It was all I could do to keep Melissa from snatching the letter from me once my mom was out of sight. She kept stretching out her hands all over the place like some kind of desperate basketball player, but I kept twisting away, holding the envelope against my chest with both my hands so she couldn't get at it.

"It's from a boy, isn't it? I knew it, I knew it!" she squealed, almost chasing me across the room.

"Melissa, this is *not* from a boy," I said, turning my back to get a closer look at the thing. My name was printed on the front in shiny black lettering, like it had been stamped there by a machine. The envelope was made out of a thick, glossy kind of paper I'd never seen before. There was no stamp and no return address. Whoever sent the thing must have just walked up and dropped it in our mailbox.

"Go on! Open it up!" Melissa exclaimed, losing patience.

I was just about to, when I noticed something printed on the back of the envelope:

TO BE READ BY AKIKO AND NO ONE ELSE

"Um, Melissa, I think this is kind of private," I said, bracing myself. I knew she wasn't going to take this very well.

"What?" She tried again to get the envelope out of my hands. "Akiko, I can't believe you. We're best friends!"

I thought it over for a second and realized that it wasn't worth the weeks of badgering I'd get if I didn't let her see the thing.

"All right, all right. But you have to promise not to tell anyone else. I could get in trouble for this."

I carefully tore the envelope open. Inside was a single sheet of paper with that same shiny black lettering:

DEAR AKIKO:
WE ARE COMING
TO GET YOU. MEET US
OUTSIDE YOUR BEDROOM
WINDOW TONIGHT AT
8:00. DON'T FORGET
YOUR TOOTHBRUSH.

And that's all it said. It wasn't signed, and there was nothing else written on the other side.

"Outside my window? On the seventeenth floor?"

"It's got to be a joke." Melissa had taken the paper out of my hands and was inspecting it closely. "I think it *is* from someone at school. Probably Jimmy Hampton. His parents have a printing press in their basement or something."

"Why would he go to so much trouble to play a joke on me?" I said. "He doesn't even *know* me." I had this strange feeling in my stomach. I went over to the window and made sure it was locked.

"Boys are weird," Melissa replied calmly. "They do all kinds of things to get your attention."

About the Author and Illustrator

Mark Crilley was raised in Detroit, where his parents sometimes wondered if he wasn't in fact from another planet. After graduating from Kalamazoo College in 1988, he traveled to Taiwan and Japan, where he taught English to students of all ages for nearly five years. It was during his stay in Japan in 1992 that he created the story of Akiko and her journey to the planet Smoo. First published as a comic book in 1995, the bimonthly Akiko series has since earned Crilley numerous award nominations, as well as a spot on *Entertainment Weekly*'s "It List" in 1998. Crilley lives with his wife, Miki, and their son, Matthew, just a few miles from the streets where he was raised.